SAVE ME
A SINGULAR OBSESSION NOVELLA

LUCY LEROUX

TITLES BY LUCY LEROUX

The Complete Singular Obsession Series
Making Her His
Confiscating Charlie, A Singular Obsession Novelette
Calen's Captive
Stolen Angel
The Roman's Woman
Save Me, A Singular Obsession Novella
Take Me, A Singular Obsession Prequel Novella
Trick's Trap
Peyton's Price

The Complete Spellbound Regency Series
The Hex, A Free Spellbound Regency Short
Cursed
Black Widow
Haunted

The Rogues and Rescuers Series
Codename Romeo
The Mercenary Next Door
Knight Takes Queen
The Millionaire's Mechanic
Burned Deep - Coming Soon

Writing As L.B. Gilbert
The Complete Elementals Saga
Discordia, A Free Elementals Story
Fire
Air

Water
Earth

A Shifter's Claim
Kin Selection
Eat You Up
Tooth and Nail
The When Witch and the Wolf

Charmed Legacy Cursed Angel Watchtowers
Forsaken

CREDITS

Cover Design: Robin Harper

http://www.wickedbydesigncovers.com

Editor: Deidra Krieger
www.kriegerediting.com

& Cynthia Shepp
http://www.cynthiashepp.com/

Thank you to all of my readers especially to Jennifer Bergans for her editorial comments. And thanks to my husband for all of his support even though he won't read my sex scenes!

CHAPTER 1

"This wound is healing nicely," Dr. Eric Tam said, squinting at the mostly-closed hole in the billionaire's arm. He kneeled down on a Persian carpet that probably cost more than he made in a year.

Eric was in Oxford, England. He had been sent by his employer, Calen McLachlan, to check on his friend Gio Morgese after the man was hurt saving his fiancée, Sophia.

Though he was from Rome, Gio was currently living in England to be close to her. Their home was a luxury penthouse in the center of the city.

He'd met quite a few of his boss' friends but not the Italian banker he'd gone to school with. So far the man was as kind as his reputation. He was certainly being very patient considering this checkup was largely unnecessary. The banker had an entire team of medical staff at his disposal.

"That's what my doctor said," Gio replied, with a faint smile on his face, but he wasn't looking at him. His attention on his fiancée, who moved around in the kitchen behind Eric's back. "Calen didn't have to send you all the way out here," he added, watching Sophia with a slightly dazed expression.

"It's not a problem," Eric assured him. "He just wanted to make sure you were okay since he couldn't fly out to visit himself."

He was about to explain what was keeping Calen in Boston, but decided not to bother. Gio wasn't listening to him. Eric didn't blame the man for his distraction. Sophia, a curvaceous Hispanic woman, was the definition of a Latin bombshell.

He turned his head briefly to find the woman in question had also stopped what she was doing when she sensed Gio's gaze on her. The two shared a private glance filled with a heat so intense, Eric was surprised his hair wasn't singed in the crossfire.

Across the room, Sophia blushed and put her head down. Feeling warm himself, he turned back to Gio, focusing on putting a clean bandage on his arm...but a heavy weight started to collect in his chest. It grew until it was too difficult to ignore.

Andie.

He hadn't thought about her in months—had forced himself not to. Seeing Gio and Sophia share a private moment brought it all back. Overwhelmed by a wave of pain and regret, he tightened the fastening on the bandage too much. Hurrying to fix his mistake, he readjusted it until it was perfect.

"Are we done here?" Gio asked softly.

He glanced up to see his patient's golden-brown eyes were on him now. Though Gio was still being polite, he could feel the man's frustration to be alone with his smoking hot fiancée.

Eric coughed. "Of course," he said, trying to think of something else to add. When he couldn't, he focused on gathering his gear.

Since his physician's assistant had taken a job that required less travel, he had to pack up his equipment on his own. It wasn't a problem this time. His medical bag wasn't big. Working solo was only an issue when he needed to have special equipment shipped out, like a sonogram or portable x-ray machine.

Gio stood to walk him to the door. "Thank you again for

coming all this way. I told Calen it wasn't necessary, but he insisted."

"It was no problem," he repeated. "I was just across the pond in France doing health insurance exams for Calen's new restaurant employees in Paris."

"Are you exclusive with McLachlan Inc. now?" Gio asked as they crossed the expansive foyer.

Warming to the subject, he nodded. "I am. I left the concierge service I was with when he threw his support behind me to start my own. I'm supervising a few other docs. We tag team to cover all of Calen's clubs and restaurants. He prefers to handle his staff's healthcare needs personally, rather than having them solely depend on local resources. Calen is our only commercial contract, but we keep busy with a lot of volunteer efforts as well and will be expanding to the Caislean group next year. I spend a lot of time on the road these days."

Going everywhere except Vegas.

"Well, I think that's great. And I'm glad you're in a good place now."

Tensing, Eric whipped his head back to Gio. "Oh...thank you."

Where had that come from? He stared at the other man, who appeared to be biting his tongue.

Oh, no. The Italian knew about his past. Had Calen told him?

Gio reddened and put his hands in his pockets. "I'm sorry. I thought you recognized me. I was with Calen when he met you. Don't you remember?"

He didn't, not at all. Of course, he had been blackout drunk at the time. Eric shifted uncomfortably and two of them stared at each other. Half-expecting a recriminating lecture, he exhaled when Gio watched him with nothing but awkward discomfort.

"It was impressive how you saved that young man, considering the circumstances."

Wishing he could sink through the floor, Eric smiled till it hurt. "Oh, sorry. Crazy night. I don't remember all the details anymore."

Admitting that was the most difficult thing he'd done in a long while. Gio was polite enough not to dwell on his discomfort. "I'd never seen an emergency tracheotomy before. I thought there would be more blood..."

"There was some." A small amount had been on his clothes the next day.

After another long pause, Gio coughed. "Well, I've kept you long enough. Don't you have a plane to catch?"

"I do!" he said gratefully.

"Where are you heading to next?"

"Back to Boston," he said, checking the impulse to thank Gio for his time. It hadn't been a job interview.

Gio nodded at him. "*Buon viaggio.*"

"Thank you," he said, escaping gratefully. He was down the hall before his heart slowed.

He hadn't had to confront his past in some time. Down in the lobby, he asked the doorman to flag down a taxi for him. He staggered into it, throwing his bag on the seat next to him. After giving the driver directions to the airport, he slumped back in the seat, watching the city slip by.

More than two years had passed since the night Gio had referenced. After making a splash in his surgical residency, Eric had moved home to Vegas to care for his ailing mother. After she had passed, he'd stayed on because he liked the hospital he was working at. It had been a huge mistake.

His problem wasn't alcohol. It was the poker tables.

After the grinding shifts at the hospital, he started joining coworkers at the casinos to unwind. And then he started going by himself. When he had a good night he'd go to a club to celebrate. That was where he'd met Andie.

She was working at Calen McLachlan's club Lynx as a waitress to put herself through school. A light flirtation had turned into a blistering affair. They saw each other for months, whenever he could pull himself away from the poker tables.

The gambling had consumed him. His work had suffered, mainly because he started missing shifts. In the end, that had been a blessing. Trying to perform surgery after staying up all night would have been a disaster, so he didn't do it. He'd been careful to get someone to fill in at first, but his good manners and conscientiousness eroded as his addiction tightened its grip.

The hospital had no choice. When they'd finally fired him he'd gone to Lynx to drown his sorrows. The next thing he knew he was waking up with a splitting headache in the manager's office. The head of security, a huge burly guy Andie had pointed out to him, had been staring down at him with his arms crossed.

"Am I in trouble?" Eric asked.

"Not exactly." Mike Ward had laughed after introducing himself.

"Why is there blood on my shirt?"

"Because you cut a man's neck open last night."

"*What?*"

Mike uncrossed his arms. "Some stupid frat kids were daring each other to see who could swallow the most ice cubes whole. One of them started choking. Our on-call doctor tried to trach him, but he was shaking like a leaf. He was botching the thing when you pushed him out of the way. I was going to stop you, cause you were obviously piss drunk, but once you got the knife in your hand the damnedest thing happened. It was like you were instantly sober. The boss said it must have been muscle memory."

"I have done it a few times before in the ER," he admitted.

"Good thing, because you did it too fast for us to stop you." Mike said, handing him a can of soda. "Sorry, the coffee machine is in the boss' office. It's upstairs if you want some."

It was the offer of coffee that made him relax. They weren't going to sue him for practicing drunk. He could lose his medical license—and he would deserve it. He had no business treating anyone in that condition.

His relief was short-lived. "The boss wants a face to face," Mike informed him. "He'll see you here this evening, Dr. Tam."

Eric froze. *The mobster knew his name.* "Calen McLachlan wants to meet me?"

Andie had told him all about the man who owned the club. He'd thought it was amusing that her boss was the son of a notorious gangster. Well, it wasn't funny anymore.

Mike had given him a small amused smile. "At nine tonight. Don't be late."

"I might have to work tonight."

"No you don't."

"Um..."

"We know you were just fired from the hospital. And about your gambling problem. We did our homework after you passed out."

"Oh," he said, feeling sick.

Mike grinned at him. "The way I see it, you don't have many options right now. So don't be late."

And he wasn't.

The last thing he'd expected that night was a job offer, but that's what he got—after a non-negotiable stint in rehab. He'd done the latter without complaint. Getting fired was his rock bottom, but thanks to Calen he bounced back faster than he would have on his own. And he learned his lesson about judging people based on rumors.

Calen wasn't dangerous. In fact, he was the most conscientious and ethical employer he'd ever had. Eric wouldn't go out on a limb and say they were friends, but he liked and respected the man. And now, years later, he could safely assume his boss respected him. Calen wouldn't have backed his bid to open his own business if he didn't.

The one thing he did ask of him was that Eric let one of the other doctors handle his Las Vegas properties. It had been the right move. He hadn't wanted to test his sobriety or his resolve not to gamble. Years had gone by, and he hadn't returned. Calen said it was better not to tempt fate and Eric hadn't wanted to jeopardize his recovery.

By the time he got to the airport, Eric had a handle on his emotions. He tried not to dwell on the past. He reminded himself that he had done what was necessary to salvage his career and possibly his life. But it had come at a cost...and her name was Andie.

CHAPTER 2

"Did you come here tonight to see me?" Andie asked.

Eric forgot she couldn't see his nod in the darkness of the storage room.

"Yes," he groaned, pressing an open-mouthed kiss to her neck.

There had been plenty of time to stop at the club tonight since he hadn't bothered to go to the hospital for his shift.

He pushed thoughts of the hospital away when Andie giggled and her breast brushed across his cheek. Growing hard, he pulled the neckline of her tank top down, freeing one rounded breast. He palmed it, running his hand up over her nipple until she gasped.

"If they find us like this, they're going to fire you." He didn't want to stop, but felt it was only fair to warn her.

"I haven't clocked in yet, and no one but the manager knows about this storeroom," she reminded him in a whisper. He suppressed a shudder when she licked his lips with a slow stroke of her tongue. "They don't use this space anymore."

That may have been true, but they were still begging for trouble. Lynx was one of the most popular clubs on the strip. It was crowded every night. Sooner or later someone would find them here—but hopefully not tonight.

Located in the top stories of a high-rise hotel, Lynx was still the place to be despite newer imitators opening up across the strip. Eric didn't like the new places. They didn't capture the vibe this place had...and Andie didn't work at those places. She worked here.

Or she would until someone caught them grinding on the torn booth someone had stuck in a cramped storeroom.

"*Eric*," Andie moaned when his hands traced up her thighs and under her skirt. She moved down his lap, unzipping him as she went.

Drunk on the feel of her, he was slow to react when she worked his shorts down and wrapped her hands around his dick. Her tongue flicked out to tease the head of his shaft.

He hissed and held onto her head as she swallowed him whole. "Shit!"

His hips pump reflexively as she worked her mouth up and down. Each suck sent a pulse of pleasure to the back of his brain. Her hair brushed against his bare thighs, tickling him. He reached for her, his hand fisting in her hair.

It was so soft. Everything of hers was soft. Her creamy skin, her lips. Even her pussy—she was waxed smooth at his request.

But nothing beat what she felt like when he slid into her. "Stop baby," he whispered, panting slightly. "I want to be inside you."

Andie giggled when he tugged her up onto his lap. Fisting his dick, he pumped a few times so he'd be rock hard for her. He was just starting to slide into her delicious warmth when he woke up.

Eric swore viciously, rolling over in bed until he was sitting up. He dropped his head in his hands and exhaled.

It had been like this since he'd flown home. He hadn't thought of Andie for so long and now...now he couldn't get through a night without dreaming of her, of being with her. And every morning he woke up alone, aching and frustrated.

Celibacy is taking its toll.

Eric had spent the last two years rebuilding his life. Every bit of his energy went into his work and repairing his reputation as a doctor. Though female patients periodically hit on him, he kept things professional. There hadn't been anyone since Andie.

He'd reached out to the hospital staff in Vegas to make amends for the way he let them down. But not to Andie. He couldn't even explain why.

When he left, Andie gave him a brittle goodbye and then blew him off when he'd asked her to a last dinner. She didn't respond to his few attempts to stay in touch—and she shouldn't have. His one text and phone call were a half-hearted bid to keep some sort of toehold in her life. Andie deserved more.

Burying himself in work, he did his best to ignore his mixed-up feelings. Keeping busy was important. He worked eighteen-hour days and avoided temptation. He couldn't afford to backslide.

Late one night Eric had just finished clearing his backlog of emails and insurance forms when he got a call.

Let that be a wrong number. It was after two AM. Nothing good ever happened after two AM.

"Mike here," a gravel-filled voice said when he finally found his cell under a stack of papers.

He relaxed. After his inauspicious first meeting with Calen's head of security, the two had struck up a friendship. "Hey, man. How is the setup of the Sydney club coming along?"

Mike was supposed to be in Australia right now. What time was it there?

"I'm in Vegas actually," Mike answered. "We have a problem here. Andie's in trouble."

Eric sat back in his chair, a jolt of surprise and concern shooting through his chest. "I'm on my way."

CHAPTER 3

*E*ric banged on the door a third time. There was no answer. Andie wasn't home.

He'd driven to her apartment complex the minute he landed. The worn structure had grown downright dingy since he'd seen it last. Eric had only been there a few times. During their affair, he'd mostly hooked up with her at the club or at a hotel on the strip if he'd had a good night at the tables.

He knocked again, squinting through the gap in the curtains. The glass was dirty, but he could still see most of the living room. There was no furniture.

Shit. Had Andie moved?

He searched for a neighbor to question. The middle-aged guy in a wife-beater tank top next door told him Andie had given up her lease last week. He didn't know where she had gone. He tried a few more doors, hoping to find someone who had her new address, but no one else answered.

Giving up, he headed to his rental car, taking the steps two at a time. Once there he texted Mike to ask if she had updated her employment records. The answer came right away.

No, that's the current one in her paperwork. There's more news now. Calen has decided to let her go.

They were going to fire her? What for? Andie had been one of Lynx's best waitresses for years. She had gotten the job there so she could go to school in the day, and never missed a shift when they had been together. As far as he knew she had done a stellar job—as long as no one knew about the two of them hooking up in the storeroom. And he didn't think anyone did.

No one but Mike knew they had even been together, and that was only because Eric had told him. They'd bonded after spending weeks working together setting up Calen's new restaurant in Dubrovnik. After a particularly long night they'd been having drinks and Eric had finally shared the details—minus his and Andie's storeroom activities.

The news taken the other man by surprise. Mike was a hell of a security chief. If he hadn't been aware of their relationship, then Eric was confident no one else knew. Andie hadn't seen fit to share the news with any of the other waitresses. According to Mike, she never mentioned him at all. Eric tried not to think about that.

Throwing his jacket into the passenger seat, he sat behind the wheel before texting Mike again.

What the hell is going on?

It wasn't the first time he asked, but the security chief had been strangely silent on the matter. All he'd said was that the situation was still developing. Eric didn't like the sound of that.

His phone buzzed.

Get over here to the club's security office. It's bad.

He swore under his breath, driving to the strip as quickly as he could.

The interior of Lynx always appeared strange to him in daylight. The dark interiors were a little washed out, and it lost a little bit of its magic. However, it was oddly more intimidating at this hour, with its leather and ultra-modern light fixtures and moldings. Calen spared no expense on details people only got hazy glimpses of at night, With the lights on he could see the detailed designs on the moldings and the texture on the walls.

I am not cool enough for this place, he thought as he climbed the stairs to Mike's office. The security chief had sent a follow-up text. Calen was joining them. Whatever this mess Andie was in was pretty fucking serious.

His heart dropped when he opened the door to Mike's office. Calen was already there, sitting behind the desk. Mike, a burly guy with silver in his hair, stood next to him. He pointed to something on the computer screen in front of them.

"I don't see it," Calen muttered. He looked up and scowled. "What the hell are you doing here, Eric?"

He hesitated. Hadn't his boss known he was coming?

"I called him," Mike said.

"Why?"

The question hung in the air for a second. Eric resisted the urge to apologize as he sat in the chair on the other side of the desk.

"I trust his expertise over the others in the new medical crew," Mike said. "This thing is about to blow up and I want our best hands on deck. Plus, he and Andie were friends back in the day."

"Really?" Calen asked, narrowing his eyes at him. "*Just friends?*"

Eric nodded, grateful Mike didn't go into detail. Disclosing the true intimate nature of their relationship—*former relationship*—probably wouldn't help her right now.

"Now can you tell me what's going on?" he asked Mike.

The security chief and his boss exchanged a loaded glance. Calen sat back in the leather chair, taking something out of his pocket and setting it on the desk. It was a clear capsule with a purple liquid almost neon in color.

"This is Drek. It's a new designer street drug. Some variant of liquid heroine, but with a supposed smoother high. It's highly concentrated and can be hidden anywhere. You swallow the capsule whole or it dissolves in a drink before you can blink. We got wind of it only a few weeks ago but it's all over the strip now. There have been two ODs at other clubs so far. One kid is in the hospital—a complication from an undiagnosed heart issue. But given how fast it's spreading, this is only the start. These things are so tiny some drunk asshole's going to pop a handful any day now. I want to get out ahead of this before someone dies here."

"Okay, but what does this have to do with Andie?"

Mike stepped back and hit a spot on the panel behind him. A molded square opened, revealing a hidden wall safe. Eric tried not to stare open-mouthed at the high-tech set up as he hit a few buttons and opened the door. Mike took out a small plastic bag holding a bunch of identical neon purple capsules.

"We found these in Andie's locker during a random spot check."

Bullshit. He shook his head. "That can't be right. She doesn't do drugs. She barely even drinks. I don't think I ever saw her drunk the entire time I lived here."

He didn't care how much time had passed. That wouldn't change.

Calen raised a brow. He gestured to the baggie. "This isn't recreational use. This number of pills can only mean one thing—she's dealing."

Eric's mouth opened, but it took him a minute before he found his voice. "I don't believe it. Given her family history, she wouldn't go near this kind of shit."

His boss's expression grew even more suspicious. Calen could read people very well, and Eric wondered how long he could maintain the fiction that his interest in this was purely out of concern for a friend.

"And what history is that?" Calen asked in a neutral tone. "Andie doesn't even have an emergency contact on file."

Crap. Trust Andie not to have confided in anyone. *And how could she not have an emergency contact?* She had a ton of friends. Didn't she have anyone she could count on?

Eric took a deep breath. He was violating a confidence, something she had told him during a late night pillow talk session. But he didn't have a choice.

"Look, she wouldn't want this spread around, but Andie told me her mom was a junkie. The woman would get clean and then slip over and over again. Andie spent her childhood bouncing around different relatives' houses and the occasional foster home."

He leaned forward. "Andie was careful to downplay it, but it really affected her. She was on her own from the age of sixteen, a firsthand witness to how drugs can wreck someone. It made her more determined to finish school and pursue a career."

"That doesn't mean she wouldn't deal to make some extra cash," Calen pointed out. "I pay well, but college is expensive."

Eric wasn't convinced. "It just doesn't seem like her. This job was putting her through school. It pays more than any other place on the strip, right? I don't think she'd jeopardize her place here doing something illegal."

Despite his reputation, Calen was an exceptional employer. Eric was proof that the man took care of his staff. Calen passed a hand over his hair roughly. He looked tired. "The stuff was found in her locker. Drug affiliation of any kind is grounds for dismissal. It's in the contract every single member of my staff signs. My hands are tied unless we can prove these belong to someone else."

Mike coughed, and finally decided to weigh in. "I think there's some room for doubt. Andie's worked here for years and except for her 'friendship' with this ass, she's basically a good kid."

Calen huffed a laugh. "I know she's a nice girl. We've never had an issue before according to the manager. She's a high earner tip-wise, but it's up to the police to clear her. And honestly, I don't see that happening. Not if they think they can track this back to someone bigger."

"You've turned her over to the *police?*" Eric choked out.

Calen's mouth turned down. "Not yet. But I don't think we have a choice. The local cops have been in touch with all the nightspots on the strip. There's an alert asking for any information on Drek. Someone is coming by in an hour to pick this shit up."

"So they don't know about Andie's involvement yet? Couldn't we just withhold the information for a day or two? Long enough to find out who this stuff really belongs to?" he asked.

Mike winced. "What do you want us to tell them? That we know who the dealer is, but we're giving her a few days to clear her name?"

Eric sat up straight. "She didn't do this. And *you're* going to clear Andie."

"Me?" Mike asked.

"Yes!" Eric turned to Calen. "I know you aren't convinced Andie is innocent, but I am. Which means you still have someone—most likely another member of the staff—who is dealing this shit behind your back. That person must know where the security cams are located, since you haven't mentioned catching anyone in the act."

Calen and Mike exchanged another glance.

"I'm right, aren't I?" Eric asked. "You haven't caught anyone dealing. Not even Andie. And she's probably all over the footage serving drinks and doing her job. All you have is this baggie, which could have come from anyone."

"There was only one possible interaction where she may have slipped a patron something extra along with their drink, but the camera angle's off," Calen said. "It could have been an extra napkin for all we know. But the staff lockers have unique combinations. She already told us she hasn't shared hers with anyone else."

"Another person could have found her combination out easily enough," Mike pointed out. "All they had to do was watch her open it. Most people aren't suspicious enough to keep their locks covered when they put in their combination."

Eric leaned forward. "So you confronted her with this?" he asked for confirmation.

Mike nodded. "I called her into the office last night, right after we finished the inspection. I put her on immediate probation while we sorted this out and told her not to talk to any of the staff on the way out."

"Does she even know she's fired yet?"

"She has to know it's coming. The rules are clear. Zero tolerance."

"Will you at least agree to keep her name out of it when they come to pick up the drugs?"

"*No.*" Calen's face could have been carved from stone, but he must have seen the dismay in Eric's expression because after a moment he softened. "Look, I have a zero tolerance policy for a reason. I don't need to give the cops a reason to be more interested in me or my business than they already are. The best I can do is tell them there's a strong possibility the stuff was dumped in Andie's locker by someone else."

Of course. Calen's family ties to the Irish mob made him an automatic suspect in just about every crime the authorities couldn't solve. His resolve to keep everything above board was the only reason he didn't have law enforcement riding his ass twenty-four seven.

"That's good enough for now," Eric replied, injecting his voice with as much gratitude as he could while still hoping for another concession. "But I still think we need to keep investigating other suspects. You said you wanted to get ahead of this. Finding the stuff in Andie's locker isn't an open and shut case. It's too easy."

Mike grumbled something that might have been some sort of agreement, but Calen steepled his hands and appeared to be thinking it over.

"What exactly did you tell the police when you called them?" Eric asked, turning to Mike.

"Just that we found some of the stuff they were asking about. Nothing else," he said.

Eric tried not to appear too hopeful, but Calen rolled his eyes at him anyway. "We say we found it in the bathroom, behind one of the toilet tanks. Meanwhile, we look into it some more. But I can't give Andie her job back. Not until she's cleared." He stopped to point at Mike. "Get on that. I trust you more than the cops to handle this."

Well, that hardly needed saying. With few exceptions, Calen kept a high wall of lawyers between him and most members of law enforcement.

"Maia and the baby are waiting for me at the Caislean 21," Calen added, naming the boutique hotel his friends, the Tyler brothers, had opened off the strip. "We'll be staying there until this is resolved."

Eric stood up to follow his boss to the door. "I'm there too. And thank you again for keeping an open mind. I'm sure Mike will be able to clear Andie. She *is* a good person."

Calen gave him another narrow-eyed glance and gestured for him to follow him to the hallway. "Look I appreciate you watching out for a *friend*, but I don't want you here if it's going to threaten your sobriety," he said bluntly.

"I haven't gambled in years," he protested.

"And you haven't been back to this town in all that time. You haven't been tested." Calen put a hand on his arm. "I don't want you here if it's going to set you back. You're a grown man and I'm not going to tell you what to do. But please think about leaving if you start to feel the itch to place a bet."

"Trust me, gambling is the furthest thing from my mind."

"Just promise me you'll go home if being here starts pushing your buttons. Mike will watch out for Andie. And if he vouches for her and continues to believe she's innocent, then so will I."

Eric inhaled and nodded. "I appreciate that, but I really am good right now. I don't think my being here is going to be a problem. I should have come back sooner."

If he had, then he'd know where Andie was right now. Maybe none of this would have happened.

Calen nodded before leaving. Eric watched him go, feeling he had done the best he could for Andie so far. As long as Calen was willing to give her the benefit of the doubt, then she'd have a real chance of getting out of this.

Turning back to the security office, he offered to help Mike in whatever way he needed.

"Just stock up on your anti-overdose drugs and be here tonight," Mike said. "I'm assigning some of our off-site security personnel to go over this camera footage and flag whatever is suspicious."

"I will," he agreed. "Do you have any idea where Andie might have gone? Her neighbor said she moved out last week before all of this happened."

Mike pursed his lip, looking at him from under surprisingly thick lashes. "She might have moved in with her boyfriend."

An actual punch to the gut couldn't have surprised him more. "Oh."

It's been forever. Of course, she's moved on. He cleared his throat. "Do you have a name for him? An address maybe?"

"Yeah, but there's not much point heading out there now with rush hour traffic starting. He'll be in for his shift at eight."

"His shift?"

"Todd's a bartender."

"Okay. Was he around a few years ago?" The name rang a bell. He thought he remembered a bartender named Todd. A handsome guy with brown hair. *Popular with the ladies.*

"Yeah, he was around. You would probably recognize him if you saw him. Used to be a swimmer. Has a few tats."

It didn't sound like the guy he remembered. The guy he was thinking of didn't have any visible tats, but that could have changed since he was here last. "I want to talk to him."

"You can, but only after I talk to him. If this is an investigation, we have to treat him as a suspect. Although honestly, we've never had an issue with him either. He's one of the reliable barkeeps. He used to work at the Caislean in Manhattan."

Crap. That meant he'd been vetted. The Caislean had the strictest hiring standards in the industry. "Still, there's other people to consider. Some of them have records," he said.

Calen was a big believer in giving people second chances. Mike scoured their backgrounds to pick only those deserving of one. But maybe one of the undeserving slipped past him.

"I'm getting a list together," Mike said when there was a knock at the door.

Two uniformed cops entered the room. "Hello. Are you Mike Ward?" one of them asked.

"Yes, come in. Eric, why don't you head out to your hotel and take a nap. It's going to be a long night."

Reluctant to go now that the police had shown up, he stood slowly. Mike shot him an exasperated glare and Eric excused himself, trusting him to do as Calen promised and leave Andie's name out of this.

He detoured to the bathroom on his way out, wanting to splash some cold water on his face before getting back into his hot car.

The black marble floor of the men's room partially camouflaged the pant leg sticking out from one of the stalls. Eric blinked several times until his brain caught up and he realized the leg wasn't just lying there floating unattached in space. It was connected to a body.

Eric rushed to open the stall door. A young man dressed all in black was lying on the floor, pale and unmoving.

CHAPTER 4

Andie didn't notice the coffee mug being held in front of her at first. Wiping the tears from her eyes she squinted at Juliet.

"Sorry, I'm such a mess. I just can't believe this is happening. Two weeks ago everything was great. I was about to graduate, I had a boyfriend who wasn't a lying, cheating asshole, and I made bank at the hottest club on the strip. Now I have no boyfriend, no job, and I lost my apartment cause my roommate stiffed me on three month's rent."

Her friend winced. "You forgot the possible drug charges."

Her stomach roiled. "Oh God. Do you think they'll report me to the cops?"

"I don't think they have a choice," Juliet said, sipping at her own mug. "Do you want me to ask Mike when I go in?"

Juliet was also a waitress at Lynx. She wasn't a close friend, but she did owe Andie her job. The younger woman had been good friends with one of Andie's cousins. They had both grown up in Las Vegas, but Juliet had a rougher time of it than Andie. She had gotten kicked out of her house as a teenager for being gay, and had bounced around friend's houses or in shelters.

Technically, Juliet hadn't been old enough to work at Lynx when she applied. All the staff had to be over twenty-one, but she had gotten a fake ID somewhere. She asked Andie to put in a good word for her with the hiring manager, which she had done. It had been a small gesture on her part, but Juliet was still grateful—enough to give Andie a place to crash since her roommate had bailed on her.

It was a good sign that Juliet was willing to talk to Mike. She had gone through some bad shit at the hands of the men in her family, and Mike was an intimidating motherfucker until you got to know him. Andie was still a little bit nervous around him, but he had obviously earned her friend's trust.

Andie leaned back on the beat-up couch. It was an alley discard, but as street couches went she'd slept on worse. "Thank you, but if they're going to the cops then I should do something now, right? Like go talk to them."

Her friend held her mug closer. "In my experience, going to the cops and expecting them to help you is a bad idea. Maybe getting out of town for a while would be better."

Andie rubbed her face. "And run away? I get what you mean about the cops, I really do, but if the shit is about to hit the fan maybe I should get out in front of this."

Juliet raised a brow. "You think the cops are going to believe you when you tell them the drugs just showed up in your locker?"

"I hope so. I mean what else can I tell them? I don't have a record, and I have a degree now. Or at least I will when I pay my last outstanding library fine. That has to count for something, right?"

Juliet didn't look convinced. "It would be better still to give them someone else to suspect."

Andie's brow creased. "Like who?"

"Like Todd, the shithead you caught banging another girl in the bathroom," she said, crossing her arms. "He was pissed when you broke up with him wasn't he? He would totally do something vindictive like this to get back at you."

Is she serious?

"They weren't technically banging. Not yet." Andie tapped her nails against the coffee mug. "You don't think he'd do something like that? Todd's not into drugs. He still swims like fifty laps a day. I've never seen him do anything stronger than shots. He's one of those my-body-is-a-temple douchebags."

Juliet nodded, "Just because he likes to exercise doesn't mean he's not selling shit or isn't above some sort of petty revenge. Doesn't he have your locker combination? Cause I think I saw him opening it once."

Andie drank more coffee. "Did you? I don't know anymore. I don't think I gave it to him, but I never changed it from the default one Mike gave me, even though he told me I could. I guess I should have. But even so, I'm not sure Todd is the one who did this. He wants to get back together. He's still texting me, trying to convince me what I saw in the bathroom was totally innocent."

"And you buy that? You already suspected him of hooking up with other girls. Why else were you dropping in on your nights off?"

Andie stared down into her mug as if contained all the answers. "I was trying to catch him cheating," she admitted. When she finally had, she'd broken up with him right away. But it was long overdue.

Todd had jerked her around for so long about so many different things—where they ate, what she wore, who she talked to. She wasn't a doormat, however, and she tried to call him on his shit when it came up. But Todd had this knack for convincing her she was the one in the wrong. He was so skilled at it, her thoughts had grown so muddled, she had started to doubt her right to question him.

There was a word for that. *Gaslighting*. She'd written a paper on it in college, and felt like a fool when she realized she had been experiencing it for months—albeit in a less extreme form.

I'm done with those fucking head games. Maybe she should give the police his name. Todd could be out for revenge.

"I'll think about mentioning him." If he hadn't done it, she was doing him a major disservice. He may have been a crappy boyfriend, but he wasn't a criminal.

"Think hard," Juliet said, pointing at her. "You have to look out for yourself, cause in my experience no one else will." She put down her mug and checked the time on her phone. "I should jump in the shower and get ready for work."

Andie winced.

"Sorry." Juliet wrinkled her nose. "I'm sure you'll get your job back. Or better yet, you can start searching for jobs in nursing."

"I'm trained as a physician's assistant. It's not exactly the same."

"Well, it's medical. Maybe getting fired will turn out to be a good thing. You can throw yourself into finding something in your field now."

"Yeah, maybe," Andie said, trying to sound more optimistic than she felt. She didn't mention how badly depleted her bank account was. That would seriously hamper any sort of job search.

And if I get charged with a drug-related offense it all goes away. She'd never be able to get a job working in medicine. "I'm going to get dressed too. I think I have to go to the police station. Now."

There was an urgency building in her. She had to make sure she wasn't going to go down for something she didn't do.

Andie left at the same time as Juliet, but the urge that sent her to the police station to file a report dissipated the longer she waited to speak to an officer.

Determined not to waste time, Andie sat on a hard plastic chair and took out her phone. She started making a list. The first few items were things she might be able to sell. Juliet was willing to let her crash for as long as she needed, but Andie paid her own way. At the very least she could contribute to groceries and the utilities.

Her cell phone bill would be due soon too and she needed to keep it active. Without it all her job prospects were dust.

The wait stretched and eventually her mind wandered. She glanced down at her notes and her heart dropped to her knees when she read what she'd mindlessly typed—*Call Eric.*

Oh, hell no. She deleted the note and shoved the phone in her pocket.

She wasn't going to get in touch with him. Not after all this time. Andie swallowed and blocked the mental image her brain had just thrown up, but it was a particularly vivid one of Eric's head buried between her legs.

Squirming in her chair, Andie flushed while fighting tears. It had been two years, but it still hurt to think about him. Recklessly in love for the first time, she'd done things with Eric she still regretted.

I was a completely different person back then, she reminded herself. Everyone had one person they went completely stupid over. Dr. Eric Tam was that person for her. But he was in the past—and he was staying there.

Andie ground her teeth, trying not to think about him. Which meant he was the only thing on her mind now.

When Eric had first started coming to Lynx as a regular she'd been immediately infatuated with him. He was tall, with broad shoulders and movie star good looks. She'd gone so far as to bribe another waitress to give her his table. After a night of determined flirting, he'd made sure to sit in her section whenever he came back. One night she had "bumped into" him in one of the dark corners of the club. He'd wasted no time taking her up on her unspoken offer. They had jumped into a physical relationship that night, her very first.

Images of wild lovemaking in expensive hotel rooms flooded through her...dancing and having sex on the roof of the hotel... hooking up in the storeroom. Sucking him off in the bathroom— which to her shame had been *her* idea.

He didn't even realize you were a virgin your first night with him. She hadn't told him.

Andie had been in her early twenties and worried he would find her inexperience gauche. But she hadn't wanted anyone enough to get physical before. Not until she met him.

Eric lived up to her every secret desire and expectation for a first lover. Soon she was like an addict, panting after him like a sex-crazed lunatic.

Stop it.

In the end, the man of her wet dreams had left her in the dust like everyone else in her life. It didn't matter that she loved him. It was over and done with. And the only salve to her savaged pride was the fact he had no idea how deeply she cared for him. She never told him and he never asked.

Men were idiots.

Juliet was right. Andie had to watch out for herself. Getting up, she marched back to the reception desk. "I've been waiting for almost two hours and I really need to make a statement about a bunch of drugs found at Lynx last night."

That got their attention. She hadn't mentioned the club when she'd first come in, but everyone here must know about Calen, the club's owner, and his ties to the Irish mob.

Within minutes she was ushered to a private office. There she wrote out a statement, giving them Todd's name, and explaining how she thought the drugs got into her locker.

Yes, she was throwing her ex under the bus. If he hadn't done anything wrong, he had nothing to worry about. And if he was the one who'd planted those drugs in her locker, then the cops were the least of his worries. She would kill him herself.

CHAPTER 5

"Is he going to be okay?" Calen asked Eric as he checked out the patient lying in the hospital bed.

The OD Eric found in the bathroom had been identified. He was a local college kid who'd come to the club with friends. The others assumed he'd hooked up with a girl he'd been eyeing and took off with her. He hadn't been missed till the next afternoon.

"He should pull through," he assured his boss, checking the student's chart once again. "It's just a good thing we found him when we did."

Overdose drugs had been administered as soon as he'd been able to get his kit from his car. It had been touch and go there for a while, but the young man had pulled through. His parents were flying in from Colorado to take over his care.

Eric had stayed all night at the local hospital—his former workplace. It had been awkward as hell at first, but the staff didn't seem to hold any of his bad behavior against him. It was a credit to their professionalism that they didn't boot him out on his ass when he walked in. It helped that the ER staff had changed in the few years he'd been away. There was always a high turnover there.

Also, the fact his "mobster" boss was around might have also helped with greasing the wheels with the hospital administrators. They'd gone out of their way to welcome him when they learned he was there.

Calen saves me yet again.

He turned to the man in question. His employer looked as tired as he felt. There were dark circles under his eyes and his hair was mussed for the first time in memory. A few years ago, Eric would have guessed he was worried about the viability of his business, and how this overdose would affect his bottom line. He knew better now. Calen genuinely cared about people, whether they were his staff or just customers.

"You should get back to the hotel. Maia is probably worried about you. And given the situation back home, she shouldn't be left alone."

Calen acknowledged his advice with a tilt of his head, but his eyes didn't leave the kid in the bed. "I asked one of her other friends, Peyton, to come with us so she's not on her own. And I don't want to take Maia home just yet. I will, however, get out of here as soon as Mike arrives. It's only a matter of time before the cops show up to take your statement. I'd rather they meet me at the club when my attorney is present."

"Which one is on standby?" Calen had *a lot* of lawyers.

"Lee."

Eric nodded. "I'll make sure the hospital staff keeps me updated. If anything changes with his prognosis, I'll call you."

"Sounds good."

He stepped into the hallway and spoke to the charge nurse about his request.

"Sure thing," she said with a bright smile and a flutter of her lashes. Eric blinked and glanced at her name tag. Nurse Ellie. Was she the one who had started calling him Asian McDreamy?

He decided she was when she winked at him. He nodded politely and retreated back down the hallway, embarrassed.

Mike stood at the open door of the patient's room next to two men. One was a short Hispanic male. The taller one was an African-American woman, whip-thin with a no nonsense expression. Their suits screamed plainclothes detective.

"Eric." Mike waved him over. "This is the doctor I was telling you about. Can you tell the detectives about finding the student?" he asked, gesturing behind them.

The room was empty save for the patient. Calen had ducked out ahead of the cops' arrival. Eric launched into an explanation, briefly detailing his position and how he'd treated the overdose.

The woman, who only gave the last name Carter, did all the talking. She asked several questions and then proceeded to shock the hell out of him.

"Are you acquainted with Andie Simms?"

He stared at her blankly, hoping he didn't appear as shocked as he felt. "Yes, why?"

Carter flipped to another page in her notes. "Miss Simms came into the station earlier today to make a statement about some drugs being found in her locker. Is it the same drug this boy OD'd on?"

"Possibly," he said, trying to cover his confusion.

Andie had gone to talk to them voluntarily? That had to mean she was innocent. He checked Mike's reaction, but the big man was expressionless. Eric was the one giving everything away on his face.

He redoubled his efforts to imitate Mike's stoicism as the rapid-fire questions continued. He had the faint sense they were trying to trip him up, but they didn't ask him the one thing that would have thrown him—about his personal relationship to Andie.

"Did Miss Simms mention where she was staying?" Mike asked. "We understand she left her old place recently, but she forgot to update her address with the club's manager."

Carter straightened and narrowed her eyes faintly. "She did, but we're not at liberty to disclose it," she said in a noticeably colder voice.

Oh, great. The cop was going think they were searching for Andie to shut her up or threaten her in some way.

"All right," Mike said dismissively. "I'm sure she'll come in to pick up her next check."

Eric nodded in agreement, although he hated not knowing where she was. Eventually, the cops left and he and Mike were alone with the patient again.

"If Andie went to the cops to make a statement, then those drugs are definitely not hers," he said emphatically.

"Not necessarily," Mike replied. "She could be trying to throw them off the scent. But I admit it's not likely. We are inspecting the other members of the staff."

"Is there anything I can do to assist?" He'd do anything to help her. Maybe a big gesture would ease the abruptness of his departure two years who.

"I'll let you know. I'm going back to the club now to set up a few more cameras—discreetly. In the meantime, get some rest. You look like death warmed over, Asian McDreamy."

Eric flushed and wrinkled his nose. "Where did you hear that name?"

Mike laughed, but he sounded tired. "You still have fans here I guess, despite flaking out on them. The nurses have been whispering like mad at their station."

How awkward. "I only care about one girl's opinion. I need to find Andie."

"Ask Todd," Mike said. "Just don't do or say anything stupid. Everyone's a suspect."

"I won't tip him off about the investigation," he promised. "I'm only going to ask if he has Andie's current address."

I won't ask if she ever mentions me or if she's happy. And I won't ask if she loves him...

There were some things he was better off not knowing.

CHAPTER 6

*E*ric was at Lynx before the doors opened. He let the manager, Trey, know he was on call as their doctor that night, but he had a few questions for him first.

"When does Todd start his shift?" he asked.

"Todd K or Todd S?" Trey asked, shuffling through some papers on his desk.

"I don't know. Which is the bartender?"

Trey smiled. "Both are. But only Todd K is on the schedule today. He should be prepping at the main bar now."

"Okay, good. I need to ask him something," he said, hurrying away before Trey asked him what it was.

The main room of Lynx boasted an open space with stairways on three sides. Two led revelers to a catwalk where they could dance. The third led to the VIP suites.

Those were the rooms where Andie would serve celebrities and casino high-rollers. Once upon a time, that last group had included him. Now his access to those exclusive spaces was because he was the on call doctor.

That is how it should be, he reminded himself. Eric had never wanted to be a high roller. He'd just wanted to gamble. It was the thrill he was addicted to, not the perks that came with winning.

He paused at the bottom of the stairs, taking inventory of the main room. Lynx was such a big club, there were actually several bars. But this central space had one so special, magazine articles had featured it.

The main bar had been custom built to suit the décor. A circle of cloudy steel with built in lights gave it the illusion of floating in space like a UFO. The massive glass top, with its softly rounded edges, had required special craftsman as well. There were no stools. Instead, black leather couches surrounded on two sides a little distance away, while the third side was unobstructed. There the floor inclined down until it opened onto the dance floor.

The bar was so large it had to be manned by at least four bartenders. Two, a man and a woman, were currently behind it arranging glassware and cutting garnishes for the assortment of drinks they would serve later.

"Are you Todd?" he asked stepping closer to the male bartender.

The tall brunette man stopped in front of him, setting two glasses on the bar.

"Yeah, that's me." He cocked his head at him. "Don't I know you?"

He shrugged. "Maybe. I'm Eric, one of Calen's concierge doctors. I used to be a regular when this place first opened."

The guy nodded, the defined muscles of his arms straining against his white cotton sleeves as he polished a whiskey tumbler. "Oh, you're Andie's ex," Todd said with a smirk as he set down the glass and picked up another. "What can I do you for?"

Wondering why the guy wasn't more worried about her, Eric leaned against the bar. "Mike filled me in on her situation. Apparently, she recently moved out of her apartment and didn't leave a forwarding address. He would like to know where to find her. Is she staying with you?"

Please say no.

"*Mike* wants to know?" Todd asked with a laugh. It was a normal enough sound, not smug, but it made Eric want to punch him in the face.

"I would like to say hello as well," he said evenly. "I'm going to be in town for a while at Calen's request."

Mentioning the boss was less than subtle, but it got the dick to give him an answer, albeit grudgingly.

"Me and Andie are on a little break right now," Todd said, moving off to stack more glasses. "You know how she is. Blows up hot and then simmers down. It's kind of our pattern, but she always comes back. We're actually thinking of moving in together."

The hell she is fuckwit. "So you don't know where she's staying right now?"

Todd pursed his lips. "Couldn't say. You might want to check with the other waitresses. She's friends with all of them." He finished stacking more glasses and leaned back to check his stocks. "I have to grab some more bottles in the back. Sorry, I couldn't help you track down Andie, but I'll be sure to tell her you are looking for her."

He left humming. Eric resisted the urge to go after him to throw the punch he'd been holding back.

You're not a surgeon anymore. Concierge medicine didn't have the same motor skill requirements surgery did. He could probably get away with a few solid punches.

"He was fucking with you, you know."

Turning, he was surprised to see a young nondescript woman watching him. She was wearing the Lynx waitress uniform—a black minidress with silver trim.

They used to be silver with black trim. Andie had been devastating in that outfit. Of course, everything looked amazing on her.

"I'm sorry. I didn't see you there."

"Don't worry about it," the girl said. "I'm used to it. My name's Juliet. And Todd knew exactly who you were. Andie still keeps a picture of you on her phone. He used to give her shit about it, but she wouldn't delete it."

"She didn't?" He tried not to sound as pathetically happy as he was. "Do you—"

"She's staying with me. Off Highway Fifteen, Kenwood Avenue, number four-o-three, apartment ten. I'm only telling you this cause of the shit she's in. If you fuck with her more, I'll fuck with you," the short blonde said with a deadpan expression. "Is that clear?"

The address was close by. He could be back in less than an hour —before the club got going for the night.

"Crystal clear. Thank you so much," he said, already heading to the door.

Juliet put her hand on her hips. "She won't be happy to see you."

"I know."

CHAPTER 7

"Motherfucker!" Andie slammed the door shut.
It is not Eric Tam on the other side of the damn door. Of course, it's not him. You've hit rock bottom and now you're hallucinating. Doc Hotshit is long gone. He left you eating his dust instead of his cock.

"Andie? I know you're not happy to see me... That's okay. I just want to talk and your roommate, Juliet, told me you were here."

Juliet wasn't her roommate. She was crashing on Juliet's couch. Roommates paid rent. She had no money.

Crap! This was not supposed to happen. Not like this. She was supposed to run into Eric in New York or Paris after getting engaged to an attractive, wealthy man. Someone who dwarfed Eric's six feet. *Maybe an NBA player.* She would be wearing the perfect red dress with her hair and face expertly made up. Eric wasn't supposed to show up when she was both homeless and jobless, dressed in a tank top and a pair of boxer shorts with the elastic shot.

"Can I come in?" he called through the door. "I can wait till you get dressed. Mike was concerned about you. Are you okay?"

Oh God, this was humiliating. Not to mention her brief glimpse of him was enough to confirm Eric was as tall and gorgeous as she remembered. He was even dressed neatly in a button-down shirt rolled up at the cuffs despite the crippling afternoon heat.

Damn him and that fucking effortless style. Why couldn't he have gained weight or started losing his hair? *You don't have to open up.* Being an immature brat was always an option.

"I'm not going away until you talk to me."

Sighing heavily, Andie pulled away from the door and went to her bag to grab a pair of jeans. When she finally opened the door she was composed and wearing her cutest I'm-not-trying-to-look-good-outfit. And shoes. Being barefoot always made her feel more vulnerable. Well, right now her feet were covered in black leather steel-toed boots. It was as strong and confident as she could get on short notice.

Eric gave her a small smile. "Hi."

She stared at him with what she hoped was a withering expression.

"Mike called me about the pills they found," he said after an awkward silence. "I realize it's been a while, but I was worried about you. Do you want to talk about it?"

This was either some sort of dream or a nightmare. "Are you serious? I haven't seen you in *years*."

He blinked and shook his head. "I know it's been a long time. I'm sorry. But this is the first time I've been back in Vegas since I left. I did call and text when I was able to."

She had wanted to be cool and casual about the amount of time that had passed before he'd reached out to her, but his reminder set her off. "That was *months* after you left. And those pills weren't mine. I even went to the police to tell them so."

"I know," he said quickly. "They came to talk to us at the hospital."

Andie backed away and sat at the small dinette table next to the kitchen.

"Why were you at the hospital?" she asked, wondering if he was thinking of returning to Vegas and getting his old job back. Did he expect her to see him again if he did?

Eric glanced around, looking adorably flustered at the lack of seating. The only other chair at the table was full of books, so he remained standing.

"I found a guy passed out in the bathroom of Lynx after hours last night. An overdose. We suspect it was Drek. He had a few more capsules of it in his pocket."

Andie felt her stomach drop. "*Oh*. Is he dead?"

"No, I found him in time. Needless to say, the cops were pretty interested in the pills Mike found. He doesn't think they were really yours by the way."

She covered her face with her hands. "Doesn't matter. I know Mr. McLachlan's zero tolerance clause backwards and forwards. I've read it a dozen times since I got dismissed."

"You're on probation. You're not fired yet."

"I'm not fired up until the point I get arrested," she said. "I'm not sure they believed me when I went to make my statement."

"Calen and Mike are going to keep searching for other suspects. I just wanted you to know that. I'll be staying around for a few weeks as well. And if you'd like another place to crash, you can stay at my hotel."

She lifted her head up out of hands, prepared to blister his ears with swear words bad enough to make a sailor blush, but Eric forestalled her.

He held up his hands. "In your own room, of course. Far away from mine. On a separate floor. Whatever you like."

Biting her tongue, she counted to three. "No thank you. I'm fine here."

Eric nodded slowly. "Okay."

He put his hands in his pockets and she waited for him to say he had to leave, but he just stood there fidgeting with something in his pocket.

LUCY LEROUX

"Well, thanks for checking in," she said impatiently. "You can leave now."

"I was in rehab."

"*What?*"

One hand came out of his pocket, gesturing aimlessly at nothing. "I left so abruptly I didn't have time to explain." He swallowed and averted his gaze. "Wow. I imagined this conversation over and over, but it's harder than I thought." He looked back up to meet her eyes. "You're surprised. I guess you didn't suspect?"

Andie belatedly realized her mouth was open. She'd been around a lot of drug users in her youth, but Eric hadn't rung any of those warning bells. And she prided herself on being able to spot a user from a mile away.

"What were you on?"

Eric shook his head. "It was poker actually…although I was starting to drink pretty heavily there at the end, after I started losing. When I left I had lost almost everything—even my mom's house." He coughed. "I supposed I should be grateful she didn't live to see that. She still thought I was a successful surgeon when she died."

Andie remembered he'd told her he'd moved back to Vegas to take care of his sick mother. The woman had passed before she met her, though, and Eric hadn't liked speaking about her after she was gone. She tried to think of something to say, but Eric was intent on getting his explanation out.

"I had pretty much hit rock-bottom that night I did the emergency tracheotomy. You heard about it right? I had just been fired, lost the last of my cash and my car. I came to Lynx to drown my sorrows. I was hoping to see you, but to this day I'm glad you weren't there. I don't remember much of what I did, but it's my rock bottom. Not remembering still freaks me out. I'm just grateful I pulled it off and didn't kill the kid choking. I attracted your boss' attention with that stunt. The next day he offered me a job, one contingent on going to rehab and moving out of Vegas permanently.

Except for leaving you, it was an easy choice. Or at least I thought it was at the time. I didn't realize how much I would miss you."

Shit! I don't have to forgive him.

"You could have told me all of this years ago," she pointed out.

He rubbed the bridge of his nose. It was a familiar gesture. He'd done it a lot those last few weeks before he left.

"I was ashamed of myself. I mean, I *lost* my mother's house. I still can't believe I did that. But you're right. You deserved an explanation—a better one than I just got a job offer I couldn't turn down. Although, in my defense, back then I still believed Calen was Irish mob. I was scared of him so I may have rushed to rehab."

"And they didn't have phones?"

"Not for the first month. Part of the rules."

Damn it, was she allowed to be mad after hearing his explanation? The first call from him had been around a month and a half after he left.

You can be whatever the hell you want. She didn't owe him anything.

"Thank you for explaining, but all of this isn't really relevant. I admit I've hit a rough patch, but I'm confident the cops or Mike will clear me. As for our former relationship, there's not much to say. We used to hook up. Now we don't. We've both moved on."

"I haven't."

There was a charged moment when her heart did a little loop-de-loop.

"There hasn't been anyone since you and I ended things," Eric continued. "I know you have someone in your life or did very recently, but I didn't want anyone else. I was focused on getting better and more recently on building my business. I'm running my own concierge medical service now. We work exclusively for McLachlan properties, but we're going to branch out soon. I'm hiring more staff as we speak."

Andie felt like she was encased in ice while her mind raced, trying to decide what to feel. Was he hinting that he wanted to get back together or was he trying to recruit her for a fucking job?

My dream job, she reminded herself.

Wait, he doesn't even know you decided to become a physician's assistant. She'd gotten her acceptance letter for the UNLV program right after he left.

"So...you've been busy," she said lamely.

"I missed you," he said softly. "I still do."

Fuckety fuck fuck.

Andie stood up. "I don't know what you want, but I can't deal with this right now." Her priority was to stay out of jail and find a job.

And it wasn't like he was *asking* her to get back together. All he'd said was he missed her, nothing more. That was some grade A passive-aggressive shit. She wasn't going to put herself out there again. Getting her heart smashed to pieces once was enough.

She started to move to the door, so she could open it and ask him to leave, but he grabbed her arm.

"I still want you," he said in low, intense tone. "That hasn't changed. But I can't live here anymore. Calen was right about that. When I leave I'd like you to think about going with me. My home base is in Boston. It would be a fresh start for you too. You've never liked living in Vegas."

Her mouth dropped open. *Unfuckinbelievable.* "You should have asked me two years ago!"

"Andie, I couldn't have taken care of you. I was a bad bet back then. Plus, you were still in school."

Man, he was a gambler. A bad bet... How had she missed that?

"First off, I can take care of myself. Second, you should have told me what your situation was. We were...we were..."

What the hell had they been to each other?

The hottest thing that would ever happen to her. A fantasy she dreamed up. After all this time none of it felt real, despite the fact he was standing in front her now.

Eric's grip on her arm tightened and he drew her closer. "We were this," he whispered.

A buzzing started in her ears, and she watched him wide-eyed as he reeled her in. Then his lips touched hers.

A supernova of heat blew through her. It was just like in the movies. One second she was a normal human being, the next she was a boneless pile of mush clinging to him as his mouth consumed hers.

This wasn't a sweet nice-to-see-you kiss. Eric didn't make any allowances for the time that had passed. His lips weren't soft. They were hungry, ravenous, robbing her of her willpower and good sense.

His hands ran down her back and up her sides. They passed over the sides of her breasts until her nipples were hard and tingling. She pressed the aching tips against his chest. The cotton of her shirt and bra were thin enough for her to feel the texture of his shirt as she rubbed against him.

Eric groaned and carried her to the floor. Her heart was racing, her breath coming in short pants and gasps. The sound of a zipper filled the air and then she felt the rough texture of carpet under her thighs.

Blood rushed from her head, the space between her legs heating and swelling. Incoherent cries filled the air, stopping only when she bit her lip.

Then he nipped her clit through the cloth of her panties and she sobbed aloud. It wasn't too hard, just right. Then her panties were gone, skimmed down her legs by Eric's beautiful hands—the hands of a surgeon.

She was squirming, restlessly pumping her hips, trying to get closer to his touch, but Eric pulled back, stopping to stare at her bare cunt.

"I love how wet you get," he whispered, leaning closer to blow on her heated folds.

He inhaled deeply as if to draw her scent into his lungs. Whimpering, she reached out and pulled his hair.

"Don't worry," he said. "I'm going to take care of you—starting now."

His tongue snaked out, licking her up and down, seeming to relish her taste. He nibbled on her clit, stroking her with his mouth and hands. His tongue probed her entrance, teasing her with a series of quick licks. Her hips rose to meet his mouth, trying to deepen the penetration, but he continued to torture her, only peeking into her with frustratingly shallow strokes.

"Oh God, *please.*"

Eric hummed in satisfaction before pushing into her with two fingers. He pumped in and out while his mouth fastened on her clit, sucking in time with his rhythm. Andie writhed on the floor, lost in the climbing heat.

He'd done this before. His talented mouth and hands had driven her crazy many times, but it had been so long ago. She missed feeling this way. Being with Todd was nothing like this—their sex life had always been about him. He'd never stirred her blood the way Eric could.

One touch from the doctor and she was wet and ready, every nerve ending straining in anticipation.

The rhythmic movement of his mouth and hands ignited an answering pulse in her blood. She clamped her thighs around his head, trying to pull him in even closer. But his hands held her down, forcing her still as he consumed her like a starving man.

The ceiling above her started to fade in and out as her pussy began to pulse in time with Eric's hands and mouth. His tongue thrust deeper, delving into the heart of her and she splintered, edges of light appearing in the cracks of her soul as she exploded in his arms.

CHAPTER 8

"*I hate myself.*"

"Why?" Eric sounded hurt.

His long, hard form was currently wrapped around her naked body on the floor of Juliet's apartment. He was still fully dressed, his hardness pressed against her backside. She'd fully expected him to unzip and fuck her brains out.

The truth was, she wanted that to happen so badly it hurt. But Eric had restrained himself, pleasuring her without taking anything for himself. Under the circumstances it was chivalrous. Any other guy would have gone all the way. It's not like she would have said no.

Andie was feeling sorry enough for herself to tell the truth. "You show up and I fall into your arms like some sort of sex-crazed idiot," she said, turning away as the recrimination built up inside her.

It felt like someone was sitting on her chest.

"Andie, you're not crazy and you're not an idiot." He shifted to stare down at her face. "We have something. It's deep and strong.

The fact it's still here after all this time apart means it's never going away. Come to Boston with me. We can live together, and you'll find a job you like. Maybe Calen will take you on at one of his other clubs or restaurants. Or he can recommend you to the Caislean chain. I'm sure he'd be willing to once this drug mess is cleared up. I know it won't be perfect with my travel schedule, but you can come with me whenever you're able to. I'll buy you a ticket anywhere I'm going."

It sounded like a dream come true, but she had been burned too many times in the past. Her dreams didn't come true. She had learned that lesson the hard way. White knights didn't appear out of the blue no matter how badly you needed them.

Two years was simply too long. All her dreams of happily ever after with this man had died long ago—right around the time she had stopped waiting for him to come home. Shortly after she had started dating Todd.

"I think you need to go now," she said in a low voice. "This is over. It has been for a long time."

Avoiding his eyes, she picked up her discarded clothes and started pulling them back on and stood up. *Don't cry. No matter what you do, don't cry.*

Eric moved to his knees, stopping her hands as she tried to zip up her jeans. He tugged on the open flaps to pull her closer and pressed a soft kiss above her mound on the skin of her belly.

"I regretted not asking you to wait for me," he said, looking up at her. "But I thought you deserved better. That was always in the back of my mind—in rehab and when I went back to work. I'm *still* not good enough for you. There is probably some billionaire out there who you're supposed to be with. Someone like Calen. But they can't have you. You're mine and I *am* going to find a way to make this up to you."

Eric stopped to nuzzle that spot on her belly again. "Someday my child will grow here," he whispered.

Her breath caught, tingles running up her spine as he stared at her with eyes that glowed like coal.

"I love you, Andie. Once you understand that—after you forgive me—I'm going to be here," he said putting his hand on her stomach and stroking down until he reached her pussy.

Tugging her waistband lower, he slipped his hand inside the band of her panties and stroked her clit briefly before moving down and pushing into her with his fingers.

"I'm going to fuck you hard and often, filling you with my seed. I want to see you get big and round with my baby and then I'm going to fuck you some more knowing *I* did that to you. And then I'm going to point you out to every man I see and I'm going to tell them, '*See that gorgeous pregnant woman? She's mine.*'"

Annie's mouth was gaping open, her lips parted as Eric's other arm snaked around her, cupping and kneading her ass to press her closer. She grabbed his arm for support, her eyes rolling back into her head as he continued to fuck her with his hand.

She should have pushed him away and slapped his face. But she didn't. Instead, she widened her stance so he could take her deeper.

The shrill ring of the doorbell snapped her out of her euphoria.

"*Shit!*"

Eric paused, glancing at the door uncertainly. Andie pulled away and fastened her pants, running to the kitchen to wash her hands and splash some water on her face before returning to the living room.

She flushed, well aware the scent of her arousal filled the air. The impulse to ignore it was overwhelming but the shrill buzz filled the air a second time.

Eric crossed his arms, apparently content to have her scent all over his hands and face.

"Aren't you going to wash up or something?" she asked, brow creased.

"No." He slowly lifted two fingers to his lips and sucked on them, making the world spin dizzily

Holy shit, why is that so hot?

Shaking her head to clear the stupefying haze of lust from her brain, she opened the door. As it turned out it was unnecessary. The shock of seeing police uniforms waiting on the other side was more effective than a splash of cold water to the face.

CHAPTER 9

"You want me to do *what?*"

The hard-faced detective named Carter leaned forward. "We want you to wear a wire."

Andie had been at the police station for hours. At first, she had been terrified she was under arrest. The uniformed cops at her door had certainly made it seem that way—until Eric had very loudly assured he was going to call Calen McLachlan to get her an attorney ASAP. Then they admitted they just wanted to talk to her.

More like bully me...

Eric insisted on coming with her to the police station. However, they kept them both waiting so long he had to leave. Lynx's manager called to tell him there had been an accident at the club. A girl needed stitches. But Eric stayed until Calen McLachlan himself assured him one his attorneys was en route.

That had been at least two hours ago. The moment Eric left, Andie had been swept into an interrogation room. Two plainclothes detectives came in. They gave the impression of appearing bored, like they had all the time in the world. But the shorter Hispanic one kept checking his watch.

They were obviously trying to scare her into action before Mr. McLachlan's attorney arrived. She had no idea when that would be, but her request to wait for her lawyer was ignored. Meanwhile she said as little as possible. After, they left her alone again, presumably to let her sweat it out. Now they were back, grilling her all over again and the lawyer was *still* nowhere in sight.

"I don't even know if Todd is the source of those drugs," she repeated for the third time. "My friend Juliet reminded me that he knew my locker combination, but so could a lot of other people. I've worked at Lynx since it opened and I never changed it. It isn't exactly Fort Knox. I'm sure Mike, the head of security, will confirm that."

They didn't like her answer. Carter gave her a steely-eyed glare. "We can charge you right now for possession. We have more than enough evidence to put you away for a very long time. And even if Calen McLachlan's fancy lawyers manage to keep you out of jail, there's still a drug charge on your record. What hospital will hire you after that?"

Andie did her best to remain impassive, but the shock of the threat hit her like a physical blow. They had been looking into her since she made her statement, obviously searching for some sort of weakness to twist to their advantage.

Juliet was right. Going to the cops had been a bad idea.

"I haven't done anything wrong," she said hoarsely. "And I'm not going to let you push me into a dangerous situation. I may have nothing, but I'm not some nobody you can use however you want. I have never witnessed Todd using or selling drugs."

"Then *why* did you give us his name in your statement?"

"To prove someone other than me knows my combination, and he's probably one of many. Now I'd like to leave unless I'm under arrest. *Am* I under arrest?"

Carter and the chubby Hispanic man exchanged a glance. She held her breath, waiting for the bomb to drop, but at that moment an attractive ice-blonde walked into the room.

The stranger was wearing a skirt suit so sharp it could cut her, but it was the briefcase and assorted accessories that identified her as a lawyer—a very successful one.

"My client is done speaking with you," the woman said before smiling brightly at Andie. "I'm Delaney. I was sent by my employer Mr. McLachlan. Carter, Hernandez," she said, acknowledging each with a brief nod.

"We're still deciding if we're going to charge her or not, *Mizz* Delaney," the male detective said.

The Mizz was drawn out with irritating emphasis. Clearly, all these people knew each other.

"*And?*" The lawyer drawled in the same tone.

Carter stared at Andie, making her dig her nails into her own thigh under the table. She would not squirm in front of this woman.

"She can go," Carter said eventually. "But don't leave town."

Andie bit her tongue as the lawyer waved her to the door. She wanted to swear a blue streak and tell the bastards off, but she didn't. There might not be an expensive lawyer to hide behind the next time she saw the detectives.

God, please don't let there be a next time.

"Delaney," the female detective said, acknowledging the lawyer as they headed for the door.

"A pleasure, as always, Carter," Delaney said before stepping out and closing the door behind her.

"Thank you," Andie said, following the lawyer out to the parking lot. The sun beat down on her skin like a laser, but it was a welcome change. With luck, it would melt the block of ice that had grown in her stomach during her interrogation. "Thank God you finally got here. It was freaking scary in there."

"It was meant to be," Delaney said with a laugh. "And I apologize for the delay. I was in San Francisco when I got the call. I was on the next flight."

The woman had been in another state? *Damn.* "Thank you for coming all this way," Andie said weakly.

Delaney smiled her toothpaste commercial smile. "Not a problem. It's a trip I make frequently for Mr. McLachlan. And I agree those particular detectives can be pretty intimidating, but they're not bad compared to some others in that building. Carter's a ballbuster, but she's basically honest and does her job well. Hernandez would get nowhere without her."

Andie tightened her grip on her purse. "Was she being honest about having enough evidence to charge me with possession?"

"Technically, yes," Delaney acknowledged with a small inclination of her head. "But it wouldn't stick if Mr. McLachlan backs you, and Mike Ward testifies others had access to your locker. That combined with your clean record and the fact you graduated at the top of your physician's assistant program speaks to your character. I could have gotten the charges thrown out like that," she said with a snap.

"You must be good," Andie murmured, unnerved to find a stranger knew so much about her again.

Delaney reached a shiny black car, a Lexus of some type, and paused. She peeked at her sideways from under thick blonde lashes. "I'm one of many excellent lawyers Mr. McLachlan employs, but when it comes to this kind of thing I *am* the best. Which is why Eric Tam practically prostrated himself to make sure I would get to you as soon as I could instead of the lawyer on call. Now that I've seen you I know why."

Andie stared at her. "Err, why?"

Delaney gave her a knowing smile. "I recognize you. I've worked with Eric a few times as part of my job. He keeps a picture of you in his medical bag. Has it with him at all times. I asked him about it once. He clammed up and refused to talk about it. But his reaction told me plenty—enough to stop angling for a date with the man."

Holy crap! Eric turned down a date with this perfectly-coiffed Nordic goddess? Was it really because of her? Had he been pining for her the whole time they were apart?

"I need to sit down," Andie said, leaning on the car for support.

Delaney laughed and pushed a button on her keychain, opening the doors to the car remotely. "Get in. I'll drop you off at your place."

Andie climbed into the car, still feeling a little shell-shocked. "I'm staying with a friend," she mumbled, giving her the address.

She sat quietly digesting what Delaney had told her. Eric kept a picture of her with him...but he'd dropped out of her life with barely a murmur.

Her lips compressed. How dare he show up back in her life after all this time! If he had really been missing her, the ass could have called her sometime in the last two years. True, she hadn't made it easy for him by ignoring his messages in the beginning, but if he'd explained why he had to leave in the first place, she wouldn't have been so hard on him. He could have tried a little harder.

His text could have explained about the rehab. Blinking she glanced up to find they were near the hotel Eric mentioned at the police station.

She twisted in the passenger seat. "I've changed my mind. Can you drop me off at the Caislean 21?"

The blonde lawyer smirked. "Isn't that where the good doctor always stays?"

"Yes."

"Going to run into his arms and ride off into the sunset?" Delaney's smile was cynically amused.

Andie sat up straighter in the passenger seat, her hands fisting. "Actually, I'm going to kick him in the nut sack."

CHAPTER 10

*E*ric walked into the security office of Lynx with his medical kit, blood dotting his sleeve in an ominous pattern.

"Hey, can I change in here?" he asked Trey. He kept an extra shirt in his kit.

Trey gestured for him to go ahead while checking something on the video monitor in front of him. "Girl all stitched up?"

"Yes, she's fine. Just a clumsy drunk. She's part of a bachelorette party."

"She tell you why she wouldn't go the hospital?"

"No insurance. But as long as she didn't bleed out before I got here, I have no problem patching her up. What are you looking at?"

"New camera feeds. Got some in a few of the panels over the bar, installed from this floor. Mike didn't even have to wait till the place was closed to install them. Man's got skills..."

That was the second best news he'd had all day. The best had been getting Emma Delaney's text telling him Andie was released with no charges.

"Are you zeroing in on Todd Kent as a suspect?"

"One of them, yes. But he's not the only name on the list." Trey turned as Eric pulled out his spare shirt and started to change. "So I hear you went to see Andie. She okay?"

"As well as can be expected," he said, tugging on his shirt. "She got pulled in for questioning by the cops, but Delaney got her out."

Trey leaned back. "I heard. But I meant was she okay seeing your sorry ass again? It was rough for her when you left."

Eric stopped with his shirt half-open. "Did she tell you that?"

Trey huffed. "No man. I have eyes. On occasion I've been known to use them."

A heat flash of embarrassment ran over his skin. "So you knew about us back then?"

A smile played around Trey's lips. "You weren't that slick. Andie was obviously in love with someone. It wasn't hard to figure out who with...or where you went when the two of you would disappear. You're lucky the storeroom wasn't wired. We use it to store cleaning supplies now. No couch."

Oh, shit.

Trey laughed at him. "You should see your face right now."

Eric blinked several times. "Why didn't you fire her?"

Trey shrugged. "It didn't get in the way of her job. She only messed around when on break or off the clock. Some of the other waitresses have done far worse in those VIP rooms. Anything too public and I have to let them go, but I try to give them a warning first. Good help is hard to find. Especially when looking hot is a requirement."

The manager was stretching the truth on that last part. Girls dropped in all the time trying to get an application to waitress at Lynx. It was *the* place to work, but Eric guessed certain allowances had to be made for a bit of bad behavior now and again in this town.

What happens in Vegas...

"Sorry," he muttered.

"I'd say no problem, but it kind of was for a while after you left, for her. I know why you did it. Calen let something slip about your little problem a while back. I'm guessing you didn't tell Andie, though, or she wouldn't have taken you leaving so personally."

Eric sat on the couch, his hands in his lap. "She wouldn't let me explain after I got out of rehab."

"You should have had the balls to tell her sooner."

He groaned. "I know. I regret nothing more. Did you say anything to her?"

Had Andie known about his addiction before he told her?

Trey shook his head. "No, man. I found out way after and by then she seemed over it. Soon after she started dating Todd K. They seemed like an okay couple. No drama until recently."

Maybe they had no drama, but he doubted Andie and the bartender shared the passion and chemistry he had with her. This afternoon was proof their connection was still as potent as it ever was.

"You gonna nut up and sweep her off her feet this time?"

Trey did have a way with words. "Yes."

"Thought so when you showed up. Don't fuck it up this time."

Eric was tempted to laugh. "I had no idea you were so invested in Andie's happiness."

That had to be it. He and Trey weren't close.

"She's a good kid," Trey said philosophically. "This town doesn't do happy-ever-after for real very often. I'd like to see one happen for her. It's not like she wasn't preparing for one. The only missing ingredient was you coming back here."

Eric frowned. "What do you mean she was preparing?"

"You do know what Andie got her degree in right?"

Eric shrugged. "Hotel management or something? She was applying to a couple of different programs when I left. I never found out where she ended up."

Trey was genuinely amused now—a rare grin lighting his face. "She's a PA. Or she will be once she lands a job."

"A personal assistant?" Did people get degrees for that? He'd always thought it was something people fell into, but maybe an Associate degree in business would help.

The other man shook his head. "Nope. The other kind. A physician's assistant. Just like in the TV show about the concierge doctor. I think she was getting ready to work for *you*—once you got off your sorry ass and came back for her that is."

Eric's head snapped up. It felt as if someone had just hit him with a brick. Then he exhaled in a whoosh. "That is literally the best news I have ever heard!"

Andie had chosen a career that would enable her to work at his side. And he needed a PA at this very moment!

Was it a simple coincidence? Had Andie liked the idea of helping a doctor in the field or was it as Trey described? Had she devoted two years of her life to a field of study in the hopes of someday working close to him?

It took rigorous study to become a PA. Holding down a full-time job on top of that must have taken discipline and strength of will.

I can't let her lose it.

A drug charge, even the suspicion of association with illegal drugs, would complicate all her future job prospects. All of her work would be flushed down the drain. They had to find out who planted those drugs in her locker and permanently clear her from this cloud of suspicion.

"Can I help you monitor the cameras?" he asked, feeling pressed to do something.

"I am on the live feed. Mike took the backlog of the normal security feeds to the company apartment. He's hoping someone slipped up in the past."

"Must be like a needle in a haystack."

Trey humphed. "Worse. It's a needle in a stack of sweaty writhing bodies, some of whom bring their own needles in with them. Catching an actual deal going down is going to be hard when the cameras have captured plenty of recreational drug use over time. It's the kind of normal shit that happens in clubs. Viva Las Vegas and all that shit."

"So I just sit and wait?"

Trey shrugged. "You want me to comp you some drinks?"

"Hell, no."

Calen would have let a drink or two pass. It was a club after all. But staying away from the poker tables required vigilance. Eric couldn't afford to deliberately weaken his will-power.

"Then I guess you sit and wait," Trey said, giving him the side-eye.

Trying to hide his frustration, he sat on the couch, taking out his laptop. He pulled out the financial prospectus for his new company, but couldn't focus on it.

It would be too late to go see Andie after he was done here and he didn't have her new number. He'd given her his before he left the police station, but had been too flustered to ask for hers. *Dammit, that had been stupid.*

"Could you stop doing that?"

"Doing what?" he asked, belatedly realizing he was tapping the keyboard rather loudly. "Oh, sorry."

Trey smirked and reached over to the desk phone. "I'm calling Suzie. She's a nurse who does the weekend shift here. Once she gets here, you can go."

He sighed in relief. "Thanks, Trey," he said, his whole body relaxing.

For the next half-hour he counted the minutes until the nurse came to relieve him. Then he was out the door like he'd been shot out of a cannon.

CHAPTER 11

Andie uncrossed her arms and sank deeper into the couch, fingering the fine cloth underneath her. She had been sitting in the lobby of the Caislean 21 for over an hour and was starting to feel stupid.

Across the hall the security guard walked past her, giving her a hard glance. He'd been doing that a lot since she came in and realized Eric wasn't there. He was at the club working and probably wouldn't arrive till dawn. But she had no cash for a cab and was too stubborn to get up and leave. Not to mention, the bus didn't stop anywhere near here.

The Caislean 21 only had twenty-one guest suites. It was incredibly exclusive.

Eric must be doing pretty well to stay here. According to rumor, the hotel frequently turned away celebrities.

She stared at her hands self-consciously, feeling distinctly out of place in the chic interior of the lobby.

"Drink?"

Andie blinked, startled to find a man holding a tray next to her. There was an ornately finished glass holding a golden brown drink.

"Is that—"

"A sidecar," he finished. "Calen thought you would like it."

Her mouth dropped open and she searched the lobby for the imposing figure of her boss.

Former boss—who apparently knows my drink preferences. Sidecars were what she always drank after her shift ended at the club.

"It's okay. Calen went upstairs. His wife needed him."

"Oh." She stared at the man holding out the drink. He was young, a few years shy of thirty, and very handsome.

"Our bartender does a good job on these, I promise."

The stranger must work for the hotel, she decided, tentatively reaching out to take the drink. When she did he gave her a big grin.

"I'm waiting for someone," she explained, wondering if he was going to hit on her. He looked a bit familiar. Had she seen him at the club?

"I know," the stranger said, continuing to give her a bright charming smile. "And I decided to give him a little break by liquoring you up first."

Andie blinked at him. "Excuse me?"

"The person you're waiting for is in for it," the man laughed. "Calen suggested you might be here to say thank you for a favor, but I know that look on your face. It's the same one my sister gets when her husband is about to be read the riot act. I thought I'd help the poor shmuck out with a little liquid relaxer."

Andie narrowed her eyes, but the man continued to smile until she almost felt like smiling back. Slowly she lifted it to her lips and took a sip.

"If you need another, let me know."

With that, the stranger left her sitting there alone and confused. But she finished the cocktail. A good sidecar was not in her budget these days. Who knew when she'd be able to afford one again? She continued to study the now-empty glass until a uniformed waitress came and brought her a second one. Then she drank that one too.

"Wake up."

Andie started when someone shook her. The brown-haired man was bending over her. He stood back and gestured with a tilt of his head.

Eric was hurrying past the lobby and climbing into the elevator. The door closed before she got to her feet.

"I'll have to walk you past security," the man said.

"Oh, thank you."

She only saw one security guard, but he wasn't giving her the evil eye anymore. Not with this man at her side.

"Hi Tom," her helper said. "This young lady is headed to the guest suites."

The formerly hostile guard nodded. "Any friend of yours, Mr. Tyler."

"Actually, this is a friend of Dr. Tam's," the man said, as he ushered her into the elevator.

Catching a sight of her face in the mirrored interior of the elevator, she realized her mouth was open. "You don't work here do you?"

He grinned and cocked his head to the side. "In a way I do. You can call me Trick. Everyone does."

Still sleepy and confused, she shook her head. He laughed. "Well, at least give Eric hell for me."

"You know Eric? Through Calen McLachlan?"

Trick lifted a shoulder. "I met him before he started working for Calen, at a poker tournament. And this is a little tit for tat for the rematch I'm never going to get..."

Oh. "Because he doesn't gamble anymore..."

Trick grinned. "That's right."

The elevator door opened on the third floor and he waved her out, but he stayed in the elevator. "Room seven," he said, still smiling irrepressibly.

"Thank you," she said, just as the door closed hiding him from view. She turned to the door, finding seven easily. This floor only had five rooms.

Time to get my game face on. She took a deep breath and knocked on the door.

CHAPTER 12

*E*ric opened the door, expecting the burger he had ordered, only to find the love of his life standing there with her arms crossed. He didn't need to be told she was furious.

"Andie! I went to Juliet's place, but you weren't there. I really need your new phone number," he said hurriedly, reaching out for her.

She held up a hand and walked inside, ignoring his question.

"What are you doing?"

Andie had walked over to his medkit and was rummaging through it.

"Do you need a band-aid?" he joked, wondering what she was looking for a split second before remembering what he kept in the inside pocket.

"Wait!" he called out to stop her, but it was too late.

Andie turned, with the picture of her he kept in the bag in her hand. She showed it to him and her face tightened. "What the hell, Eric? Why is this in here?"

"Because I love you," he reminded her gently.

Shaking her head, Andie looked at the ceiling as if she was

trying to stop herself from swearing. "If that was true you should have come home sooner!" she yelled before her face crumpled.

Tears welled up in her eyes and he rushed over and pulled her into his arms. "Don't cry," he crooned.

"This isn't how this was supposed to go. I'm supposed to be kicking your ass." She sniffled, trying to push him away.

Eric swore, but he didn't let go. Instead, he tightened his grip. "And I deserve that. I should have told you the whole truth, but I was ashamed of myself. But I'm here *now* and I'm going to make this up to you, even if it takes me years."

Andie hiccuped and stopped fighting him. She rested her head against his chest. "I...I should have answered your texts and calls back then."

"You didn't have a good reason to," he admitted, fitting her under his chin and holding her closer. "I should have left you with more. It's just I was afraid you weren't as serious about me as I was about you."

An unexpected kick to shin made him wince. "You are an *idiot*."

"Not anymore," he said, wincing. Moving his hands to the side of her head, he pulled her in close to press a determined kiss to her luscious mouth.

She didn't return the kiss at first, but eventually his persistence paid off. Her lips softened under his and parted when he pressed his tongue against them.

The kiss that followed started as an ember, a slow burn that grew all-consuming. Heat rushed through him and for a moment he contemplated dragging her to the king-sized bed, but it wasn't going to be enough.

The little gasp of disappointment she gave when he leaned back was music to his ears. "I think we should get married. Now, tonight!"

Andie blinked and shook her head. "What?" Her voice was dazed.

He plunged his hands into her hair and pressed his forehead

against hers. "For once in our lives let's take advantage of the fact we are in Vegas. Let's get married right now."

She laughed and shook her head again. "That's crazy."

"That's what this town is for," he pointed out, pressing her tighter against him. "Be young and crazy for once. Marry me tonight."

Frowning she looked down at her clothes. "No. I can't. I came here after sitting in the police station for hours."

He grinned. "I have a solution. The concierge here is amazing. He can get anything in under an hour. Meanwhile, you can jump in the shower."

Letting go for a moment, Eric reached for the phone. "Hi, this is Dr. Tam in room seven. Can I get a wedding dress delivered to my room ASAP?" He broke off. "What's your size baby? An eight?"

"Yes," she said, her eyes wide.

"Eight it is. Yes, great idea, thank you. No, a sapphire solitaire I think. Yes, at least four karats." He hung up the phone. "Done!"

Andie's mouth was open. "You got a ring too?"

"If you don't like it we can get a different one later. I would give you my mother's ring, but it's not very nice."

"This is unreal," she said. "I need to sit down."

He led her to the bed, kissing and caressing her lightly until she took him up on the offer of a shower. After she was done there was a knock at the door.

The dress and ring were delivered in forty-three minutes, which had to be some sort of record. It was, however, long enough for Andie to change her mind about marrying him three times—not including the time spent in the shower. He had to use every weapon at his disposal to change it back but she crumbled the instant he held up the beautiful gown they had delivered. It was a simple sheath of the finest satin, with a skirt that fell to the floor in a cascade of shimmering light.

Less than an hour later, they were married by an excellent Elvis impersonator—Andie wanted a traditional Vegas wedding. She giggled the whole way down the aisle, but grew serious when he promised to devote his life to making her happy.

"Everything that I am, everything that I ever will be, is for you," Eric vowed. "I love you."

Andie's smile lit up the room. "I never stopped loving you and I never will. God knows I tried."

He laughed and pressed his forehead to hers, more grateful than he could say for the second chance he'd been given.

The rest of the ceremony was a blur. In fact, nothing was clear until they got back to the hotel, bursting into the room only to find it transformed.

There were flowers everywhere. Ornate arrangements rested on every surface, and a mix of rainbow petals littered the bed. Next to it was a bucket of champagne, a plate of chocolate-covered strawberries, and two champagne flutes.

"Oh my God, did you order this when I wasn't looking?" Andie asked.

"No," he said, barely noticing the décor as he went for the zipper of her gown. "It must be a gift from the hotel."

Nibbling the soft skin of her neck, he peeled down the silky fabric, aided by a shimmy of her hips. Too impatient to remove anything else, he picked her up and they landed on the bed.

Andie's hands helped tug off his clothes and soon both of them were naked, crushing the delicate flower petals underneath them.

Eric scooped up handfuls of the satiny confetti. He piled them on her body, unsure which was softer—the petals or her skin. Andie sighed and picked up more, rubbing them against his bare chest and pulling him close, trapping the fragrant petals between their bodies.

Time blurred as he explored the length of his new bride's body. He kissed every inch clear of petals, and shifting the ones in his way when a particularly delicious spot was covered.

His hands moved a little roughly at first. It had been too long and he wanted her too badly. She didn't complain, but he made an effort to check himself before he marked her creamy skin.

Touching Andie was like coming home. He knew her body almost as well as he knew his own. His hands remembered every line, every curve, and dimple. His tongue explored the hollow at the base of her neck, working his way down until he was licking the indentation of her hips before shifting to the side to delve deeper still.

Writhing underneath him, Andie's whimpers turned to moans as he licked the hot flesh between her legs. Stroking and probing, he let his memory and instinct guide him. He pushed her harder and faster until she was straining, her hips pumping as she gave herself over to the pleasure.

He ate her with abandon, teasing her with his hands and mouth until she shattered, crying out and squeezing his head between her legs. Using his strength, he pushed himself up, stroking the sensitive skin on her inner thighs with his torso before positioning himself at the entrance of her pussy.

"I love you," he said, taking himself in hand and teasing her, running his hard cock over her clit.

"Please, Eric," she whispered, breathing hard and tugging on his shoulders to bring him closer.

Holding her hips, he entered her, forcing himself to go slowly, to savor the sensation. Pushing past her little opening, he slid inside, her hot clinging sheath enveloping him tighter than any glove.

A broken ragged sound escaped his chest. He bent to kiss her lips as he slid home, rocking into her, trying to cover all of her body with his. She rose to meet his body but he pinned her down until she couldn't move. Instead she clung to him, accepting his thrusts with a series of little gasps, her whole body tensing as her orgasm washed over her.

Andie's climax triggered his own. He held on a few more precious seconds, closing his eyes to savor each ripple and spasm, but he couldn't stop or delay any longer. He rocked into her hard, grinding his hips as his cock jerked, spilling his seed into her waiting womb.

Eric collapsed, holding onto Andie's hand until he recovered enough to shift to the side. "Don't move," she said reaching out for him.

He smiled and slipped his arms around her, pressing his face into her hair. "I didn't want to crush you. That was literally the best thing I have ever felt in my entire life. And not just because I've been celibate for so long."

Andie giggled before her mouth turned down and she frowned. "I'm sorry I can't say the same. I should have waited for you—for this."

Eric shook his head. "I didn't ask you to. I didn't have the right and you shouldn't feel bad there was someone else. We were apart a long time. And it's better that you got a chance to experience something of the world before we got married."

That white lie eased Andie. Her frown evaporated and she pressed her cheek against his chest. "It was an empty relationship."

"Most of them are. We're lucky. And now you can tell me I'm the best lover you've ever had and I'll believe you because you've finally been with someone other than me."

Andie turned wide eyes to his. "You knew I was a virgin back then?"

"Of course I did. I am a doctor. Plus, I did a gynecology rotation."

She hid her head under the pillow. "I am so embarrassed."

"Why? It was sweet that you wanted me as your first. I knew then we had something special. I'm just sorry I was too much of a mess to make this work two years ago."

He pulled the pillow off of her head. "Why don't we have some champagne before all the ice melts?"

"Okay," she agreed, giving him a weak smile.

He stood and reached for the bottle, noticing a note taped to it for the first time. He opened it and read it, laughing a little when he saw who it was from.

"What is it? Did the concierge make a shotgun wedding joke?"

"No. It's actually from my friend Patrick. He must be here at the hotel and he's the one who chose your dress and ring. Had a lot of fun doing it too apparently—although he had help from his sister and her best friend, Peyton. He sent them pictures and they voted, so you can thank them for the gown and ring later."

Andie paused, admiring her sparkling ring. "I'll have to do something really *big* to say thank you. Maybe name our firstborn after one of them or let them garner my wages." She sat up and accepted a glass of champagne and one of the strawberries. Nibbling, her brows drew together. "Is Patrick called Trick sometimes?"

"Yes. Trick Tyler. Why?"

"I met him downstairs. He gave me a drink."

"Did he?" Eric asked with a scowl.

"Not to flirt," she assured him. "He knew I was waiting for you. Calen McLachlan pointed me out to him. Mr. Tyler thought you'd be better off if I had a few before I saw you."

He laughed. "I will have to thank him later."

"I thought it was weird until I realized he was your friend. I thought he was the concierge at first."

"Actually, he owns the hotel. He and his brother Liam."

The expression on her face was priceless.

"The Tyler brothers own the Caislean chain," he explained. "They are good friends with Calen."

She nodded. "So that's how you know them."

He sat on the bed. "Well, technically I met Patrick before when I was gambling. He's a killer at the poker tables. I only got lucky once—the last time we played. To be honest I couldn't call him a friend back then, but we've spent more time together since I went to work for Calen. Now I think we are pretty close. We even share the same birthday."

"He did mention something about a rematch he's never going to get. I hope he's not pushing you to gamble again."

"Oh no, he's very supportive. Just likes to tease. He's a pretty nice guy for a billionaire. You'll like him."

Andie tilted her head to one side. "He gave me two sidecars on the house, so I already do. You've acquired some impressive friends since I saw you last."

Eric leaned over her. "Nothing and no one made up for losing you."

Tears glinted in the corner of her eyes. "You have me now."

He nodded, a little too choked up to speak. "I do, don't I?" he rasped.

One fine dark brow went up. "So what are you waiting for?" she asked, wrapping one leg around him.

He didn't need a second invitation.

CHAPTER 13

Andie rolled over, pushing away the constricting sheet wrapped around her. But the warmth shifted, releasing her feet while tightening at her waist.

Silky fabric slid over her bare skin, leading to the sudden realization that she'd slept naked. Why had she done that? Though by no means a prude, Andie always slept in a nightgown and panties unless it was very hot. If it was, then she slept in just panties. But this morning, she wasn't wearing a stich, which was alarming enough to her muddled mind to rouse her to full consciousness.

"What?"

Her drowsy question elicited a deep chuckle from the man parting her thighs.

"Eric? What are you doing?"

Another rumble of laughter. Andie sucked in a hard breath as he lowered his head to her heated pussy. Every sensation was heightened—the tickle of his soft hair brushing her inner thighs, the way his soft lips nibbled and teased until she was wet and panting aloud.

Her heartbeat drummed in her ears as she squirmed, torn

between trying to get away and moving closer for more. He started using his teeth, gently grazing her sensitive flesh and clit in a rhythm that elicited a pulse from within.

"Eric, it's too intense." She panted, pushing him away with weak hands.

Always the gentleman, he backed off to let her recover, but she felt the loss almost immediately.

Eric kissed her inner thigh, drawing a pattern with the tip of his tongue.

"How's this?" he whispered, probing lightly before inserting two fingers. He pushed them deep inside slowly, spreading them as he went to open her further. Andie arched like she'd been shocked by an electric jolt.

This man knew her body better than she did. He found her G-spot immediately, tickling and teasing until she was crying out, pleading for more.

Skin stroked against skin as Eric swept up her body, rubbing against her until he was there, his thick length probing at her folds. At first, she thought he might not fit.

Though her break up with Todd had been recent, it had been months since they'd been together. Convinced he'd been cheating, she'd withdrawn from the physical side of their relationship long before she worked up the courage to tell him it was over.

"I missed you," Eric breathed as he slid home. Her mouth opened reflexively, gaping as the sensation of being filled and stretched set fire to her pussy's nerve endings.

As she clutched at his shoulders, her hips rose reflexively. She instinctively tried to grind against him, hungry for all the stunning little miracles that had been denied to her these past few years. But he wouldn't let her have too much too soon.

Eric held her hips. His grip wasn't hard, but it was inflexible. He used the rest of his body to coax hers into following his rhythm. The drumming of her pulse was an echo of his driving hips. He didn't let go until she was meeting him thrust for thrust—perfectly synced the way they had always been from the start.

It had never been like this with anyone else. The heat and intensity was better than any club drug could ever be.

For a second, she was angry. How could Eric have walked away from this? This wasn't just sex between two well-matched lovers. This feeling was crazy and once in a lifetime. He should have known that. *She should have known it.*

"I love you. I love you so much!" Eric reached up for her hand, the one with the ring on it. He caressed the thin platinum circle the way he ran his other hand up the bare skin of her hip and thigh. Her racing heart skipped, and she reminded herself that at least he knew it now.

And so do I.

Andie reached up and put a hand on either side of his face, kissing him. She poured everything into it—every scorching memory of their past, everything she wanted for their future.

Eric's reaction was just what she wanted it to be. His rhythm broke and stuttered, going wild. Angie held on tight, her eyes nearly rolling into the back of her head as her climax rolled over her. She spasmed around his cock, gripping him so tight it must have hurt. But she didn't let go. Her sheath throbbed, milking him as he shouted and poured liquid heat into her.

He thrust hard a few more times before collapsing on top of her.

"I'm crushing you," he said after a minute.

"I like it." And she did. His weight was welcome. They were never as close as when he was lying on top of her, spent, his seed still warm inside her.

"Still have to move," he murmured, rolling onto his back until she was lying on his chest. Eric stroked her cheek. "What do you want to do today, Mrs. Tam?"

Andie burst out laughing. "Oh, my god! I almost forgot we got *married.*"

She pulled her hand free to examine her sparkling ring. "I don't know if I can wear it every day. What if I lose it?"

"I'll get you another one," he said, pulling her close to kiss her forehead.

Andie smacked him on the arm. "Don't even suggest it. This is my ring we're talking about. It's literally the most precious thing I will ever wear. I can't lose it."

He laughed. "Then never take it off. That way you don't have to worry about losing it."

"Well, I have to take it off to shower, don't I?" She frowned at the sparkling blue stone. Just thinking about wearing it grocery shopping or while she was working made her nervous.

Eric tapped the stone. "Why? It won't melt, trust me."

She wrinkled her nose and gave him another half-hearted smack before curling up against him. "Very funny. I know what rings like this cost. I've seen lots of girls in the club showing these off, and I've heard their men bragging about how much they spent on them—more than I make in a year sometimes. And mine is more beautiful and bigger than any of those. What if something happens to it?"

Andie had never possessed anything so expensive and she'd never expected to. Now that she did, she was starting to become concerned. How did a normal person take care of something like this?

Eric read her expression. He passed a hand over her hair. "When it gets nicked or scratched—and it probably will, that's inevitable—this ring will be even more valuable. At least it will to me. Because every tiny flaw or imperfection means one more memory, more time we've been together as man and wife."

He took her hand and raised the ring to his lips. "So let it get dinged. Let its brilliance dim. It means we'll have been married for years and years."

Andie blinked rapidly. Her throat was tight. "You always say the right thing. I've always hated that about you."

He laughed, hugging her tight as he rolled until he was pinning her down to the bed. "I've been fantasizing about this day on and off for the past two years. I intend to set a record for the most insanely hot sex-filled honeymoon known to man. Are you with me?"

She wrapped her arms around him. "Hell, yes."

CHAPTER 14

Hours later, after several sex-fueled hours and a leisurely and titillating shower, they had dinner at the Caislean 21's superb restaurant. It was the finest meal Andie had ever had—a scallop and lobster appetizer and a French style *hachis parmentier* made with duck confit liberally sprinkled with *foie gras* and topped with the most buttery potatoes she'd ever tasted.

"It's a good thing we're having tons of sex or you'd have to roll me to the front doors by the time we check out."

"Well, I hope that's not anytime soon," a smooth voice interjected. "But if it comes to that, we have a full gym and lap pool in the basement."

Startled, Andie looked up. Blood rushed to her cheeks, and she stared mortified at the hotel's owner, Patrick.

"Trick!" Eric was on his feet. The two men embraced, slapping each other on the back the way macho men always did when they wanted to show affection without looking girly.

"How are you? How is married life?" The handsome brown-haired man held Eric at arm's length, a big grin on his face.

Andie didn't hear what Eric said in response. She was too busy dying of mortification.

"I have to leave for the club soon," Eric was saying when she was able to focus on their conversation again.

"Don't worry about that. Calen's got you covered—at least for the next couple of days. He told me as he was leaving."

Eric's face darkened. "Oh. Was it Maia? She insisted on going home?"

Trick's face was sober. "Yes, she did. A PI she hired thinks she has another lead."

"A viable one?" Eric asked.

The other man shrugged. "As good as all the others. Lots of women fit that description unfortunately." A flash of guilt passed over his face, and a hazy memory from last night rose. Someone was missing—a woman Eric had never met.

"I wish there was more I could do," Trick was saying, "but I have my own missing person case in a way."

He didn't sound upset, just frustrated.

"Really?" Eric sounded intrigued.

"Yeah, I'm just making the rounds at the casinos, looking for someone I played once. You're not the only rematch I'm itching for." The tone was jovial, but something flickered in Patrick's eyes.

Recovered from her embarrassment, Andie smiled wickedly. "Let me guess. This rematch you're looking for is with a woman."

Trick hesitated, then grinned. He turned to Eric. "It's really too bad you don't play anymore. This one has good instincts. I bet she would have been a hell of a cardsharp."

Andie laughed. "What makes you think I'm not now? I *did* grow up here."

She was exaggerating, of course. But she was no slouch either. Growing up in this town meant she'd played enough hands to be a passable poker player.

Both men laughed before Eric nudged Trick. "So who is this

woman? Anyone I might have met on the circuit? What's her name?"

Trick's expression shifted, his eyes widening. "That's a good question. I didn't exactly get a name, not one that gets me anywhere . Did you ever play a beautiful brunette, about this tall? She would have kicked your ass," he added, drawing a line in the air just above his shoulder to illustrate her height.

Eric's chin lifted a notch as if he was searching his memory. "There was that Japanese girl from San Diego. She was a pretty good player if I recall."

"No, that's not her. The girl I'm looking for isn't Asian. Her skin was a bit tan, but I don't think it's from the sun. She could have been white or Hispanic, but her eyes were blue."

Her husband shrugged. "Doesn't sound familiar. But I've been out of the game quite a while."

Trick clucked his tongue. "Well, it was a longshot anyway. Anyone you know from the tables, I would probably know by now too." He glanced down at their mostly finished meals. "I actually need to get going, and you need to try the chocolate mousse for desert. It's the house specialty. I took the liberty of pre-ordering it for you on the off chance you'd want to try it, but if you're not a fan of chocolate, then I'm sure someone else will—"

Andie held up a hand. "I'm going to stop you right there. I want that mousse, and I want it now."

Eric laughed. "Well, you heard the lady. But I'm going to ask that it be delivered to our room."

Andie flushed and bit her lip.

Trick squeezed his eyes shut and waved his hands. "Say no more. I'll go relay that to the kitchen and make myself scarce. Be sure to stop by the suite for a drink sometime before you check out."

"I'll do that," Eric promised, waving as the other man walked away.

"You are shameless," she chastised with a giggle as he sat back down.

He grinned. "Three words. Record-setting honeymoon."

She slid across the leather, closing the distance between them. "Well, in that case, I have a few ideas about how to serve this chocolate mousse." Andie leaned over and began to whisper in his ear.

Eric shifted in his seat. Andie giggled, looking down at his suddenly too-tight pants. She loved knowing she could do that to him with just a few softly spoken words.

Her husband waved at the waiter. "Check, please!"

CHAPTER 15

*E*ric strolled out of the shower, wearing nothing but a towel around his hips. She wanted to jump off the bed and tear it off him, but the expression on his face stopped her.

"Is the honeymoon over already?" she asked, the corner of her mouth turning up.

He smiled weakly. "I was thinking you'd liked to do some shopping while I run a few errands. You can take my credit card and hit the Strip casino shops. I hear the Venetian has a few nice ones, or maybe the Paris?"

"Don't you like what I'm wearing now?" she asked, rolling over to display her nude body.

Eric's lips parted, hunger lighting in his eyes. "I love it. If I didn't need to meet a medical supplier, I'd literally be jumping you right now."

Andie pouted and got on her knees. She reached over to run her hands over his chest. "Why don't I go with you?"

There would be plenty of time for solo errands later. And even though they hadn't worked out all the details, Andie was going to be his PA. She'd have to get to know his suppliers eventually. It would be part of her job to help with purchasing.

But Eric's expression didn't lighten. He opened and closed his mouth a few times as if trying to find the words to tell her no.

Andie backed away from him with a frown. "What's wrong? Why don't you want me to go?"

He took a deep breath. "I just think shopping would be a lot more fun. But you don't have to do that if you're not up for shopping. You can catch a movie or go to the spa. Enjoy your R and R before you start as my physician's assistant."

She narrowed her eyes at him. He might have been a better poker player, but she could still read him like a book. "What don't you want me to see?"

Eric's shoulders lowered a notch. He held out his hand. "Well, don't say I didn't warn you."

ANDIE SAT in the passenger seat of the car, staring at the modest ranch house Eric had driven her to.

She turned to him. He was watching the place with a doleful expression. "Where are we?

He leaned closer to the steering wheel, gripping it in both hands. "This is my mother's house." Eric squinted at the mailbox. "Well, it's the Sanchez's house now, I guess."

Oh. This was the house he'd gambled away.

The expression on his face was breaking her heart. She reached out and took his hand. "I would never have wanted to live here."

It worked. He burst out laughing.

"I didn't want to live here either. My mother didn't expect me to. She preferred my upscale apartment high rise, although she wouldn't consider something similar for herself. She was too set in her ways. Or at least that what she always said when I offered to help her find one."

"Then this isn't your sacred childhood home?"

"No, I didn't really have one of those." He took another long look at the house before putting the car back in drive.

"Where are we going?"

"Back to the hotel."

"I see." Andie peeked at him from the corner of her eye.

He adjusted the mirror and sighed. "Why don't you tell me what's on your mind?"

She bit her lip. "I don't want to overstep."

He glanced at her. "Don't hold back. That's not you. You've always said what's on your mind. I love that about you, so spill."

Eric was right. She'd never minced words with him, but that had been back when she'd been the girl he hooked up with and nothing more. Their relationship had been intense, but they'd never had deep personal conversations. On occasion, something had slipped out about her background. That had been inevitable. But Eric had always held back. She knew why now, of course. The fallout of his gambling and the guilt over losing everything must have eaten him alive.

But we're married now. From this moment on, they were sharing their lives. And there was something he probably needed to do before they could leave Las Vegas behind them.

"Your mom is buried here, right?"

He kept his eyes on the road but he stiffened. "Um, yeah."

"Maybe we should swing by, so we can pay our respects while we have the chance."

Eric raised one fine black brow. "We could, I suppose. But I hadn't exactly planned on it today. It's not what I would call a romantic honeymoon activity."

"I know. But I think it would be good for you. Maybe you can... talk to her or something. Get some things off your chest. At the very least, I should meet the woman so I can tell her how much I love her son."

His silence went on too long. She was starting to regret opening her big mouth when he finally replied.

"That would be...nice. Sort of." His gaze caressed her lovingly. "She would have loved you."

Andie doubted that, but it was sweet that he thought so. "Why don't we stop by somewhere and pick up some flowers?"

He nodded. "Yeah, that sounds like a plan. But just so you know, we resume normal honeymoon activities this evening."

She took his hand. "Absolutely. We have a record to break."

CHAPTER 16

Andie had never had so much sex in her life. Almost a week had passed since she'd solemnly sworn to love, honor, and occasionally obey Eric Tam.

The "occasionally" had been his suggestion. He'd said marriage would be no fun if she obeyed all the time. That was the moment she knew marrying him was the right decision.

So far she had no regrets. Even when Eric resumed working at the club, she stayed in the hotel room, relaxing with the various spa treatments he insisted she enjoy.

She also rested. There had been so many sleepless nights in the past month, and it felt good to relax and regroup before facing the world again, this time as Mrs. Eric Tam.

So many things were still unresolved. She had texted Juliet to let her know she was all right, but hadn't gone to the apartment to pick up her things yet.

Andie would be moving to Boston as soon as Eric was free. He wasn't sure when that was going to be, but she understood. He didn't want to leave Calen or Mike in the lurch while the whole drug mess was still an issue.

Eric suggested she go ahead to Boston without him, giving her license to redecorate his apartment however she wished. As tempting as the offer was, she didn't want to go anywhere without him. Plus, the cops would find it suspicious if she suddenly skipped town.

On the second evening, Andie decided to stop procrastinating and go pick up the rest of her clothes. She hadn't needed them yet, but would if she ever intended to leave the hotel again. There was a huge list of things to get done before moving.

She also wanted stop by Juliet's apartment and clean it as thanks for helping her out. Eric had given her a little stash of cash too, so she could leave some for her share of the utilities.

Andie hated borrowing money, but couldn't refuse her own husband. She would pay him back every cent, although she suspected he would fight her on that. He was very much of a *what's-mine-is-yours* mindset. Which was great, except she didn't bring much to the relationship. It made her feel guilty.

That was going to change. She had her priorities straightened out and was getting the rest of her life back in order. Once in Boston, she would convince Eric to hire her as his PA so they would never be apart again.

After her beloved groom left for the club she took a cab down to Juliet's building. She swore when she realized her phone was completely dead.

Of course, she thought as she arrived. Her phone charger was here at Juliet's. Well, if her friend had already left for her shift, at least she would come home to clean place.

Humming quietly, Andie was so busy admiring the sparkle of her engagement ring that she almost didn't notice the door to the apartment was open a crack—something her cautious roommate would never allow.

Pushing the door open with her hip she stopped short. The place was a mess. It had been ransacked. Pillows and random papers were strewn all over the floor. And it was getting worse because the person making the mess was still there.

She recognized him immediately, despite the fact his back was to her. Sensing her presence, Todd spun around to face her, a ripped sofa cushion in one hand and a knife in the other.

"What the hell are you doing here?" Andie asked, leaving the door open behind her in case she had to make a quick escape.

Todd turned around, surprise flashing across his face before it twisted. "You're so smart you fucking figure it out!" he hissed at her.

He pivoted on his heel and started grabbing the cushions off the couch, squeezing them before tossing them to the ground, swearing under his breath the whole time.

She thought she heard him say something about a *"fucking doctor"*, but she dismissed it. Then he started tearing at the lining, ripping the backing cloth from the frame.

"What the hell, that's Juliet's sofa!"

Andie stood there like an idiot as he shifted from the couch to the shelves above it, tossing things off, and opening a decorative box to check inside.

"Todd stop or I'm going to call the cops!"

She had to call the police anyway. He was vandalizing Juliet's apartment. Was this some sort of revenge for breaking up with him? He must not know she wasn't staying here anymore. Was he hoping Juliet would kick her out onto the streets so she would be homeless?

Todd flipped another table over on his way to the kitchen, where he started rummaging through the cupboards. Andie shook her head, pushing herself to do something. She fished her cell phone out of her purse, and pivoted on her heel, prepared to run out the door and call the police from the safety of the stairwell.

She stopped short, staring into the barrel of a gun.

CHAPTER 17

"You were supposed to shut up and keep your head down, but you couldn't even do that," Juliet said, the gun held steady in her hand.

Andie gaped at her, belatedly realizing Juliet hadn't been speaking to her. She had been talking to Todd.

She put her hands up in the air as if she was in an old-fashioned stick-up. "*What the hell is going on?*"

Todd whipped his head around and started when he saw the gun. "You're supposed to be at work," he said accusingly.

Juliet raised a single brow. "You won't find my stash. Look around. This isn't where I keep my money. That's hidden someplace else."

"A stash of what?" Andie was still in shock.

"The drugs." Todd sneered. "The ones she talked me into pushing for her."

Her drugs? The Drek in her locker belonged to Juliet?

The world started spinning crazily and she stumbled, but quickly righted herself when the gun swung back in her direction.

"I don't want to know anything about this so I'm just going to leave now," Andie said very quietly, holding her purse to her chest.

But she didn't make it more than a few steps. Juliet blocked her path to the door, which she must have closed behind her when Andie was staring at Todd.

"I'm sorry you got dragged into the middle of all this," Juliet said, sounding genuinely contrite. "But now that you're aware of my real business I can't let you leave."

Oh God.

"I won't tell anyone anything," she promised. "I swear."

Juliet shook her head. "I wish I could believe you. And I really did have the best of intentions when I let you stay here. I was grateful for the in at Lynx. Getting a job there is next to impossible. You're the only reason they took me on. It was hard as balls to get around Mike and the other security guys. I eventually figured out a way when I caught this asshole hooking up with a girl in the bathroom. He was a real shit boyfriend by the way. But he cared enough about you to start working for me in exchange for my promise to keep my mouth shut about what I saw. I did want to tell you, but I figured you'd find out on your own. Once a cheater always a cheater, after all. I was right too. This idiot blew up his own spot weeks later and I had an employee of my own."

"Fat lot of good working for you did," Todd muttered. "You got me involved in too much heavy shit and Andie dumped me anyway."

Juliet tsked. "Not my fault. You should have kept it in your pants."

Andie was swamped with confusion. "How did he work for you? We all would have noticed those Drek capsules switching hands. The main bar is the most crowded one in the club."

Juliet nodded. "The nice thing about those capsules is they dissolve. He just slipped one into a particularly colorful drink when I gave him the sign. It worked great so long as I was the server and the ass didn't drop more than one in. My customers would pay me direct, and it just looked like they gave me a very generous tip afterward. It was the perfect system until this shit decided to bring in the whole stash to the locker room that day instead of keeping it in his car and refilling his pockets as needed."

"So how did it get in my locker?" she asked.

"Ask him," Juliet said, rolling her eyes at Todd. But he was quiet now, perhaps unnerved by the presence of the gun. "He stuffed it in there when he heard someone coming," Juliet explained. "I told you he knew your combination."

Todd grunted. "I don't fucking remember her combination. Andie always forgets to spin the lock when she clocks in. It's almost always open during her shift."

Un-fucking-believable. She was in this mess because she forgot to turn a fucking dial?

Juliet shifted and the light reflected on the gun. *No.* She was in this mess because she had awful taste in friends and boyfriends.

Not all my choices were wrong. Eric had come back.

"I thought having Andie sic the cops on you might teach you a lesson about respect, but I guess you haven't learned anything yet," Juliet said.

"Okay," Andie said, trying to sound calm. "What can I do to reassure you I don't care about any of this? I—I just got married and I'm going to move to Boston any day now."

There was silence for a beat.

"You're *married?*" Todd exploded behind her. "You fucking bitch!"

Andie didn't turn to him. She kept her eyes on the gun.

Juliet pursed her lips. She was so quiet Andie's heartbeat picked up. Sweat trickled down her spine as she waited for an answer.

"So you married the doctor?" Juliet asked.

"Yes," she whispered, showing her the ring. Behind her Todd shuffled, but she ignored him.

"And he's friends with Calen McLachlan." Juliet bit her lip.

"Also some other billionaires apparently. I met one the other day," she added, hoping it would convince her former friend to let her go. She wasn't a nobody anymore. Someone loved her—and in a stroke of blind luck that man had some serious connections.

"Then this is going to be even worse than I thought," Juliet muttered.

Andie swallowed hard. "What does that mean?"

Juliet shook her head, an expression of sympathy in her eyes. "It means it's already too late. I work independently here, but I'm part of a network. And when this shithead forced my lock, the silent alarm I had installed went off. I called in an alert. Two enforcers are on their way. My intention was just to teach Todd a lesson. We need him to keep working the bar. But your presence here complicates things."

Andie didn't like the sound of that. She liked it even less when those enforcers showed up a few minutes later.

Juliet had motioned both her and Todd to sit on the couch. She was waiting there when two men came in. Like the bouncers at the club, they were massive, but unlike Mike and the other security guys at work these men looked dangerous...evil.

Her stomach hurt when one of them kept staring at her like she was a piece of meat. He licked his lips and she fought the urge to vomit.

Juliet pulled the men aside. They had a whispered conversation, stopping to glance up at her and Todd on occasion.

"I did this for you, pushing that shit," Todd said quietly as he sat next to her on the couch. "And then you go and marry that asshole."

Andie clenched her fist, momentarily distracted from her fear. "Eric's not an asshole. And no one told you to break the law for me. It wasn't worth it."

Todd snorted. "You got that right."

Andie wanted to turn and punch him in the face, but she had enough to worry about. Motionless, she waited for the conference deciding her fate to be over.

"You," one of the men said, pointing at Todd. "Come with me."

Todd shuffled to his feet, moving slowly toward the door. A few steps away he paused and turned back to her. "You should have just taken me back instead of marrying that fucking Jap or whatever he is."

Unbelievable. Andie wanted to laugh in his face, but she suspected if she started, she would never stop. A little hysterical bubble escaped anyway.

"He's a much better fuck," she said, with a choked laugh as tears began to fill her eyes. "Like ten thousand times better than you. Most men are, though," she added from between set lips.

If these were going to be her last words to him, or to anyone, she wanted to make them count. There would be no pleading or begging from her.

The killer near the door snorted, but Todd's face crumpled. He turned to Juliet. "Andie can dump the doc and go to work for you. Imagine how much more money you would make with both of you delivering your shit."

Andie's throat tightened, and she regretted being so harsh to him. Todd may have been a shit boyfriend but he did care about her in his way.

Unfortunately, his appeal didn't work.

"I wish that was a possibility, but Eric Tam won't understand if she wants to end things with him to return work at the club." Juliet turned to Andie. "I'm right, aren't I? Your doctor won't go away this time. Not now that you've married him."

Andie didn't say anything. She didn't have to. Juliet was so much smarter and ruthless than she had realized.

"Get him out of here."

The guy at the door shoved Todd again, hard. Before she knew it they were gone and she was alone with Juliet and the second killer.

Andie focused on her knotted hands. If she looked up at them she was going to break down, and no matter what happened next, she wasn't going to show weakness.

"He's right, you know. I could make you a lot of money," she lied, grasping at the last straw in sight. "Eric loves Vegas. I can just tell him I want to live here and he'll move back, no questions asked. I can even expand your client list through the people I'll meet being with him. He knows a lot of rich people. Some of them must like to party."

Her mouth tasted faintly of bile and she wondered if the lie had sounded as weak to them as it had in her ears.

"I'm going to go," Juliet said. Her voice sounded as if it was coming from a million miles away. "Text me when it's over."

The tears did fall then, but Andie clamped her lips shut, and refused to make a sound.

"Are you sure?" the man asked her. "I know some people that would pay a lot of money for a piece of ass like this."

"No. Her husband would never stop looking for her and he's connected to the McLachlans. We can't risk it. Make sure not to leave a mark. That means no fucking her or they'll know something else went down. I'm going to write the note now. I know her handwriting well enough."

Andie closed her eyes against the rising tide of nausea threatening to spill over.

I should never have left the hotel. How was Eric going to feel? His new bride was going to be found dead two days into their marriage.

Don't believe any lies Juliet writes, she prayed silently, hoping there was some way he could hear her.

He will know the truth, she decided, calming slightly. No matter what happened, what the note said, he would know it was all a lie. He had to.

Legs appeared in front of her. She didn't look up to thug number two, but she didn't have to. He thrust a glass of something in her face. It smelled like vodka, but it had a distinctive purple tinge to it.

"Fucking waste," he mumbled under his breath before shaking the glass at her. "Drink this," he said in a louder voice.

"No," she whispered. Andie wasn't going to help them make this appear like an accident or suicide. He was going to have to shoot her.

"I said drink *bitch*."

She shook her head. Shuddering all over, she gasped involuntarily when the cold barrel of the gun pressed against her forehead.

"*Drink*."

"*No*."

The asshole swore long and viciously, but she ignored him.

Andie put her hands around her knees and hugged them tight. Then she squeezed her eyes shut, and waited for the bullet that would end her life.

CHAPTER 18

"Why the fuck isn't Andie picking up her phone?" Mike yelled in his ear.

Eric winced, pulling his cell phone a little farther from his head. He'd just arrived at the club. It was still pretty dead, but Trey had called him into his office to discuss their ongoing security strategy.

"I think she's still at the hotel," he said, shrugging at Trey, who mouthed, "*What's up?*" "She's getting a massage later and is probably sleeping right now."

"Well call her as soon as she wakes up. There's something she needs to know. You too."

"What is it?"

"I think Andie's friend Juliet is involved in this Drek business. One of my staff just sent me a video. It's grainy but I think I'm seeing an exchange there. Todd's showing her a baggie of pills and she slaps his face and shoves them back in his pocket."

"Oh, that is weird," he agreed, sitting down.

"Yeah, and it's not some lovers spat either. Juliet's gay."

He nodded before remembering Mike couldn't see him. "I'll call

Andie right now," he promised, turning to Trey. "Are Todd and Juliet both on the schedule?"

"Just Juliet. She should be here by now. Why?"

He explained briefly with Mike still on the line. "Are you coming in?" he asked Mike.

"Yeah. We'll call the cops in and send them the video. They can decide what action to take."

"All right. I'm going to call Andie. I'll have the concierge wake her if I have to. She was crashing on Juliet's couch before I got here and was talking about going to going to get her stuff sometime this week. But she didn't mention anything about this before," he added, in case Mike decided Andie was too close to this mess.

Mike swore in a low voice. "Call your girl *now*. And have Trey get some guys to watch Juliet. Maybe we can get a buy on film."

"Okay," Eric agreed, hanging up right away. He dialed Andie's cell phone in case she'd woken up in the meantime, but when she didn't answer he called the hotel's front desk to ask them to knock on their door.

"I'm sorry, sir. There's no answer."

"Look, this may be an emergency. Can you go in with your key card? The room is registered under my name. I can give you permission."

"We will do that as soon as we have a female staff member get up here to your floor. It's company policy."

Eric suppressed a groan and agreed. He held his breath until the guy came back on the line.

"I'm sorry, Dr. Tam. It appears Mrs. Tam isn't in her room. Our records indicate she called for a cab an hour ago. She left roughly a half hour ago. The address is Kenwood Avenue."

Fuck! Andie had gone to Juliet's apartment. He hung up and turned to Trey, who was on his Bluetooth headset, talking in a low voice with one of the security guys on the floor.

"Is Juliet here?" Eric asked.

"She hasn't clocked in yet," Trey said with a frown. "Which is atypical. She's very reliable and has never been late before."

Of course, she wasn't late. Juliet wouldn't jeopardize her job as a waitress at the hottest club on the strip. Not if she was a drug dealer savvy enough to find a way to sell under Trey's nose.

"I have to go," he said, trying hard to ignore the tight feeling in his gut. "Call Mike and tell him to head to Juliet's apartment. It's four-o-three Kenwood Avenue, number ten."

"You think something's going down?" Trey asked, standing up with his phone in hand.

"I think so. Tell him to hurry."

He didn't wait for an answer before running out the door.

CHAPTER 19

Eric arrived at Juliet's apartment only a minute or so after Mike. He pulled his rented Lexus into a slot near the security chief's tricked-out Dodge truck.

"It's the one just up there." He pointed, relieved that the building seemed quiet.

Mike narrowed his eyes at the door on the second story walkway. "Were the blinds drawn the last time you were here?"

Eric frowned. "I don't think so." He glanced at the other apartments. Only the ones facing the sun had the blinds down, but it wasn't that unusual to have them down in units like these. "Do you think there's something off about that?"

"Probably not, but the reason I'm still here is because I don't take anything for granted. Wait behind me until I give you a signal."

Nodding his assent, he trailed behind Mike as the bigger man started up the stairs. Eric's lips parted as he saw his friend shift from normal man to hunter between one step and the next. Mike stalked down the hall, approaching the door on silent feet.

Eric tried to mimic his friend's fluid movements, but his medical school hadn't included black ops training. Wincing, he tried to quiet his absurdly loud breathing. Even his shoes wouldn't cooperate. They scraped on the concrete hall floor audibly as he trailed a little behind.

He thought Mike would turn and berate him, but he wasn't paying him any mind. Mike stood in front of Juliet's door with an intent expression, putting his ear to the wood before abruptly pulling back and fishing a black cylinder out of his pocket. It was a reverse peephole viewer. He fit the barrel over the lens, leaning in to put his eye to the opening.

He held his breath, waiting for an update but Mike didn't say anything. Without a word he reared back, kicking the door open with a loud splintering crack, then rushed inside at a dead run.

Startled, Eric followed. What he saw at the threshold was nothing short of his worst nightmare.

There was a man with a shaved head bending over Andie. She was lying on the floor, completely still. He didn't see a gun in the guy's hands—they were busy arranging Andie's body.

Eric's vision darkened. He barely registered when Mike flew toward the assailant. One second he stood next to him at the door, the next he was pulling the guy off her and pounding his face.

The stranger was an experienced fighter, but he didn't have the years of training Mike did. When the guy threw a punch Mike pushed, forcing him off-balance. The goon struck hard, going for the soft spots of the Adam's apple and groin to incapacitate Mike, and failing.

Mike returned those strikes with his trademark right hook, a punch so powerful it had felled men much larger than him in one blow. It didn't let him down now. He hit the guy, and the guy hit the floor and didn't get up.

"*Eric.*"

Eric blinked at him, frozen. Mike flinched, going to Andie. He yelled something Eric couldn't hear. The buzzing in his ears was too loud.

"Eric, if you don't move your ass she's going to die!"

The icy grip of shock fractured and Eric gasped, taking a huge lungful of air into his burning lungs.

"Get over here," Mike ordered, shifting to secure the assailant's hands with his belt.

Eric stumbled over to Andie, frantically checking for a pulse. In the background he heard Mike calling 911.

"Is she okay?" Mike asked.

Eric didn't answer. Mike grimaced and finished the call to emergency services before going down on his knees on Andie's other side. "What can I do?"

Eric's hands were shaking, his breath coming in short sharp pants. Mike reached out and put his hand on his shoulder. *"You need to calm the fuck down. Andie needs you."*

"Yes," Eric said raggedly in agreement. His hands were still shaking as he opened Andie's eyes to check her pupils.

He started CPR. "I need you to go to my car and get my med kit. She's been given an overdose and stopped breathing. I need the Narcan stat!"

Bending, he put his mouth on Andie's, tossing his keys in Mike's direction.

His friend jumped to his feet and ran out of the room. It felt like an eternity before pounding footsteps signaled his return, but was probably less than an minute.

Mike threw the black bag down next to them and knelt to tear the zippers open for him.

Eric's hands had stopped shaking. Indeed all emotion had been wiped away. He was on autopilot now, the years of training kicking in. He reached into the bag and had the Narcan injector assembled within seconds. Eric squeezed Andie's shoulder, plunging the needle on the thickest part of the muscle. After a beat, he resumed CPR while Mike started counting down aloud. But almost a minute passed and there was no response. Narcan usually worked right away.

Please don't let her die, Eric prayed.

"The EMTs are here," Mike said before his voice rose to address the other men. "It's okay. He's a doctor. Stand back."

The paramedics shuffled to one side while Eric prep'd a second dose of Narcan. He injected the drug in Andie's other shoulder and held his breath, willing her to start breathing again.

She didn't move, but Eric didn't stop his ministrations. His rhythmic pattern was determined and textbook perfect. He wasn't going to stop, not ever.

Somewhere behind him, the EMT's shuffled. "Should we call it?"

"Don't even think about it," Mike growled, shooting them his most intimidating death stare.

One of the EMTs actually hid behind the other one...but Mike was starting to look doubtful himself. It was all over his face—*Andie wasn't going to wake up.*

"*Yes, she is,*" he growled aloud defiantly. But inside Eric was cold to his core.

His hands were ice as they pushed up and down on his wife's chest. He didn't let himself think or feel anything. He couldn't or he would break down. If he did, he would definitely lose her.

An excruciating minute passed before there was some sign. As he lifted his lips from hers, Andie inhaled with a gasp. His may have been louder.

Eric's eyes burned as he coughed and inhaled in large gulps as if he had been the one who hadn't been breathing. Tears stung at his eyes as Andie's lids fluttered and finally opened.

"Eric?" she whispered, looking around in confusion at him and the other assembled men.

That was when he let himself cry.

CHAPTER 20

Andie groaned and shuddered.

"*Ow*," she muttered, opening her eyes to bright sunlight.

"Andie?" Eric came into view. He looked terrible. His eyes were red and puffy and his clothes were rumpled.

"What happened to you?" she asked.

He gave her a sad smile. "I'm okay. It's what happened to you that I'm worried about."

What had happened to her? Frowning she struggled to remember, noticing for the first time she was in a hospital room.

"How did I get here?"

"Mike saw Juliet and Todd on the security footage. It implicated her in the drug ring. Do you remember what happened after you went to Juliet's apartment?"

"I was going to clean it..."

She gasped suddenly. The images of a gun and those two frightening men with Juliet came to mind. "It was her," she said, numbness spreading through her chest and hands. "She told them to get rid of me."

"We know. They arrested the man who assaulted you. Mike took him down before the cops came. Your ex-boyfriend turned himself in to police and told them everything. The second man, the one who left him, is at large. So is Juliet."

"Oh...Oh my God. She had me fooled the whole time. I thought she was just a struggling waitress like me. I can't believe she was a dealer. Her place was super simple, and she didn't drive a nice car or have expensive clothes."

"Yes, the police can't find any evidence of added income. She hid her operation well."

Andie collapsed back onto her pillows. The room was spinning. Oh, God. She didn't remember what had happened to her after Juliet had left. It was all a blur, and she hurt everywhere.

"You said I was assaulted," she whispered near tears.

Eric took her hand. "Your rape kit was negative. But the man we found with you forced your mouth open to take the drugs. There's some bruising around your lips and there was residue from the spiked drink all over your shirt."

He leaned closer, pressing against her side as he squeezed her hand tighter. "I thought I lost you."

The tears she'd been holding back started falling. "I thought I lost me too. I was so scared."

"You don't have to be ever again. I'm never letting you out of my sight. I'm not even going to let you go to the bathroom alone."

Andie hiccuped and snorted a little, aggressively wiping her tears away. "You know, right now, I'm okay with that."

CHAPTER 21

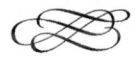

*E*ric spread the gel over his patient's extended stomach and waved the sonogram wand over it until he found the baby's heartbeat.

"Everything seems good," he told Marie-Claire, walking her through all the vital statistics for a fetus at her stage of pregnancy.

His explanation was detailed and reassuring—and completely for the benefit of Marie-Claire's anxious husband, celebrity chef Rémy Paquin. His actual patient was a rock, and surprisingly unflappable considering she was approaching the end of her first pregnancy. Next to him, Andie took notes on the vital statistics for Mrs. Paquin's file.

The chef worked at Calen McLachlan's five-star restaurant in Paris, *Meliae*. He was a brilliant culinary artist and Eric was looking forward to eating at the restaurant later that night. But first he had to get the high-strung man back to work, and that wasn't going to happen until Marie-Claire had been given a clean bill of health.

Glad he was able to give one, he wrapped up the examination without betraying his impatience to get out of there. He had a big surprise for Andie and he was eager to see her face when he gave it to her.

Months had passed since her attack. They had left Vegas immediately after getting the all clear from the cops. Her ex was serving jail time, a reduced sentence in exchange for his cooperation with the investigation.

As far as Eric was concerned, Todd had gotten off too lightly for abandoning Andie to those thugs when she needed him the most. He would have fought tooth and nail to get her away from those assholes.

She was everything to him.

The second man had disappeared without a trace, but they found Juliet a few weeks later. Her body turned up in California, in a hotel in the heart of Silicon Valley. She had been killed in exactly the same way she'd intended Andie to die—via overdose.

Despite Eric's protests, the cops in California had ruled the death a suicide. There would be no further investigation from that quarter.

Fortunately for him, Calen had Mike and his security staff continue to investigate. Mike believed any threat to Andie had died with Juliet. It was cold comfort, but it was all he had. Meanwhile, he and Andie had both started counseling, teleconferencing with a therapist they shared since they traveled so much.

Andie had teased him for his insistence on going through the counseling together in addition to her individual sessions, but he'd meant what he told her at the hospital. He wasn't going to let her out of his sight. And she didn't mind—not yet. In fact, the few times Andie had been away from him, the relief on her face when she saw him again spoke volumes.

He was determined to make sure Andie never felt unsafe again. Eric thought he had succeeded to a large degree, but the time had come to move forward. Which was why they were here in Paris. The check-up for Mrs. Paquin was a convenient excuse for their trip here, but the real reason was a belated honeymoon.

He and Andie were going to spend two whole weeks relaxing and sightseeing—without a single medical appointment scheduled till next month.

"Thank you again for humoring my husband," Marie Claire said in a low voice after her husband had hustled to the kitchen to get her a glass of water.

"It's no problem," Andie told her with a beaming smile. "We can't wait to try his food later!"

"Are you two a couple?" Marie-Claire asked glancing from one to the other.

"Yes," Eric confirmed, smiling at Andie with a heat in his eyes that made her blush. "We're married," he said with pride, turning back to his patient reluctantly.

"Oh, I remember those honeymoon days," Marie-Claire said with a laugh as she watched their interplay. "I will let you two get out of here so you can enjoy Paris."

"We intend to," Andie said, almost vibrating with excitement. She hadn't been able to sleep on the plane ride over the Atlantic, but that didn't seem to detract from her energy level.

Which is good for me. He wasn't going to need to factor in a nap before making mad passionate love to his bride.

After giving the neurotic chef his most convincing everything-is-fine speech, he gave the man a card with his temporary replacement's number. He suspected the relief doctor wouldn't thank him later. Remy would probably be on the phone before he and Andie got out of the building.

"Congratulations again!" Andie called behind her as they left the Paquin home.

"You make a great PA," he told her as they made their way outside.

Patients loved her. Andie was sweet, charming, and efficient. Her natural warmth put them at ease. They could tell she genuinely cared about their welfare.

"Well thanks, Doc," she said with a giggle. "But I think you might be a little biased. Are we really going to his restaurant tonight?"

"Yes. I hope he is too."

"Oh, I think it's sweet he's so concerned—although I hope you're not that way when the time comes for us," she added with a nudge.

"I'm going to be fine. I have a system all worked out."

"Of course, you do," she said. "You plan everything, or so I've learned since we got married." Andie stopped next to him while he texted the car service and gave him a considering look. "It's hard to believe you were ever a gambler."

He snorted. "Why do you think I ended up losing my shirt? You can't plan your way out of a losing hand."

"Well, I'm glad you got your shirt back...although I do prefer you without it if I'm being honest," she said with a wink. "Can we go see the Eiffel Tower before we check into the hotel?"

He paused at the main doors. "What if I told you we could see it from our room?"

She gasped and grabbed his arm. "*Seriously?*"

Eric smiled at her eagerness. "It's a short car ride away. Very short. I would suggest we walk, but we can't with all this gear," he said, indicating their cases.

The car eventually arrived. It maneuvered through the heavy Parisian traffic at a snail's pace, but soon the trip was over. Andie's eyes widened when she saw their location.

"Is this the Caislean Paris? Isn't it impossible to get a room here?"

"It is," he confirmed. "Which is why it's useful to know the owner. Patrick is especially proud of this place. It's their first hotel to earn six stars, but probably not their last."

He ushered her out of the cab and inside the tall granite building. The spartan exterior blended seamlessly with the lobby interior both rich and elegant without being garish or overdone. Andie whirled in a circle, taking it all in.

"I didn't know it was possible to get six stars," she said, her eyes devouring every gleaming surface and decoration.

"I didn't either until Trick told me," he replied, handing their cases over to the porter.

They checked in and went up to their suite without further delay. He unlocked the door and Andie was about to step inside when he stopped her, scooping her into his arms unexpectedly.

Andie squealed and laughed and he carried her past the threshold, setting her on her feet just inside the foyer. The grand suite of the Caislean Paris had four rooms—a sitting room, office, dining room, and bedroom. There was also a private deck with an infinity pool and hot tub.

His beautiful bride was stunned into silence. "No way!" she said after a moment, dropping her purse and running from room to room.

It was incredible. He probably owed Patrick a kidney for a suite like this.

"Is Trick going to demand our firstborn for this hook-up?" Andie asked, reading his mind after she had dashed in and out of every room twice.

"Well, I think he's working on his own right around now," he said, thinking back to his last conversation with the hotel magnate. Trick had finally met someone, although from what he'd told Eric, the situation was very complicated.

Worry about Trick later, he thought, watching Andie turn around. She sidled up to him, the shimmy of her hips hypnotic.

She flattened her hands on his chest before toying with his collar. "And what about us? Have you changed your mind yet? I can throw away my birth control pills right now..."

Eric closed his eyes as she started to unbutton his shirt. "Don't tempt me."

As much as he wanted to start a family, Andie needed time to recover from her ordeal. The added stress of pregnancy was something that could wait—at least until she stopped having nightmares.

They were fewer now, but she still woke up in a cold sweat every few weeks.

It's more like once a month now. She is getting better.

"We need a little more time to enjoy married life," he said, tracing her collarbone with his fingers. "We should revisit this conversation after our one-year anniversary…"

He had more to say, but he lost his train of thought when Andie parted his shirt, her fingers sliding across the skin of his chest.

"Honestly, I don't mind right now. I like that we're alone in this room tonight."

"Actually, this place is ours for two weeks," he said starting to nibble on the soft skin of her neck, but Andie pulled abruptly away.

"Two weeks! Shut the front door!"

He grinned and nodded. She started to jump up and down before leaping into his arms. Laughing, he spun her in a circle before carrying her through the double doors of the bedroom.

Dropping her lightly onto the king-sized bed, he started to undress, unzipping as fast as he could. But he was too slow for Andie. She pulled him on top of her with a wicked grin.

Wiggling underneath him, Andie reached inside his pants, drawing out his stiff length. She wrapped her hands around him, lifting her head to tease him with her mouth. Her tongue flicked out, licking the head of his shaft at the sensitive ridge. She scraped her teeth against it, making him suck his breath in a sharp inhalation.

He tried to pull away from her, intent on pleasuring her first. It was his pattern, part of his job. But Andie wasn't having it. Not this time. She kept her hold on him, teasing and sucking on him until he was rock hard.

Eric was close to begging when she finally let him go. Gasping, he leaned back, transfixed when Andie took hold of her skirt, slowly drawing it up. He followed it with his fingers as she exposed more and more of her creamy skin. The edge of her skirt went up and over the tops of her thighs, revealing her glistening pussy.

"Oh dear God, you aren't wearing panties." He licked his lips. Had she been naked down there this whole time?

"I took them off on the plane. I've been so wet for you all day." Her hips wriggled again, rubbing her thighs together briefly before parting them, showing him the pink lining of her lips and tight little opening.

Damn. Thank God he hadn't known until now. He wouldn't have been able to function knowing she was bare under her skirt—waiting for him. Her clit stood at attention and he pinched it, making her whimper.

"Don't make me beg," she said in a sultry voice, her eyes half-lidded as she parted her blouse and unclasped her bra.

The two cups fell away from her, revealing the pouting tips of her breasts. "Put me inside you love," he said, wanting her hands on him again.

Moaning, Andie parted her legs wider and took hold of him, rubbing his length over her moist lips and clit before positioning him at her entrance. Cupping her breast, he pushed inside slowly, giving her time to adjust to his size. She was so small, he couldn't do it too fast or too hard until she was warmed up.

Andie raised her hips, meeting him part way. "I've been thinking of this all day," she said with a little moan.

She had hidden it well. He wanted to tell her, but he couldn't speak. So he told her everything he wanted her to know with his body, the way his hands caressed her full breasts, abrading her nipples until they were peaked and stiff.

His cock eased in and out of her clinging shaft, building speed until he was fucking her hard. He buried himself to the hilt and back out again, twisting a little to hit the spot that made her writhe and cry out. He knew exactly where it was, and he didn't ever waste any time teasing her, not when he could make her come repeatedly instead.

So that was what he did. In a few minutes Andie was straining and moaning, her hands digging into his backside. She orgasmed with a little scream.

"Please, Eric," she begged. Andie tried to hold him tight, but her grip was weak. He pressed his chest again hers but kept thrusting. He was relentless. Eric wouldn't stop unless she asked...and she never had.

Moving his hands to clasp her derriere, he lifted off the bed a little, adjusting the angle to hit a different part of her. The pitch of her breathing changed and he knew she was ready for more.

"Fuck me harder—that way you do," she said, tugging on his hips.

Nearly ready to burst, he obliged, sliding into her deep and pausing when he was completely buried inside her. He ground into her hard, twisting again from side to side, a move that drove her crazy.

Annie's mouth fell open and her legs strained against him. He buried his face in her neck and held her as her body went rigid, then trembling with a deep shudder.

Her hungry little passage tightened and spasmed around him and this time, he couldn't stop the explosion. His cock jerked, jets of his seed pouring into her as he groaned, fucking her past the little aftershocks until he collapsed with a final convulsive wrench.

"Oh God, you're going to kill me," she said after a minute, fighting to catch her breath.

"*I am?* You're the one who didn't wear any underwear all day. I can't believe you were bare that whole time, and I didn't know," he said, shaking his head before laughing. "If I had known, I would have fucked you immediately—in public on the streets of Paris."

She snickered. "Then I'm glad I didn't tell you. But be warned. I will do it again. You won't know when or where, cause I'm not going to tell you. It could be a special first day in a romantic European city, like today, or the average Wednesday at home, but I will be going commando, wet and waiting for you... It'll be my little secret surprise for you."

He groaned and pulled her into his arms. "You really will be the death of me."

Andie giggled and rolled on top of him. "Hey, don't the French call an orgasm the little death?"

"As a matter of fact, they do."

She stroked his chest before tracing a letter with the tip of her finger. It was an A. "Well, I bet I can bring you back again and again and again. Just like you did me...when you saved me."

Eric took her hand, kissing her finger before shaking his head. "I didn't save you. You saved me."

And she had. He'd been going through the motions, keeping busy to distract himself from the fact he wasn't living. He merely existed, marking time until the next job.

But now he had everything. He had Andie.

The End

Need another obsession? Try Codename Romeo

Encountering a tiny toddler alone in the hall changes everything for FBI agent Ethan Thomas. Relief sets in when the child's mother appears. But when she collapses at his feet just before a blizzard hits Boston, Ethan's in over his head.

FIND this and the rest of Lucy's award-winning books using the QR codes above!

ABOUT THE AUTHOR

Lucy Leroux is another name for USA Today Bestselling Author L.B. Gilbert.

Seven years ago Lucy moved to France for a one-year research contract. Six months later she was living with a handsome Frenchman and is now married with an adorable half-french toddler.

When her last contract ended Lucy turned to writing. Frustrated by a particularly bad romance novel she decided to write her own. Her family lives in Southern California.

Lucy loves all genres of romance and intends to write as many of them as possible. To date she has published twenty novels and novellas. These includes paranormal, urban fantasy, gothic regency, and contemporary romances with more on the way. Follow her on twitter or facebook, or check our her website for more news!

www.authorlucyleroux.com